'I make it a point not to credit rumours, but it seems in this instance the rumours are true, Sasha Fleming.'

The way he said her name—slowly, with a hint of his Latin intonation—made goosebumps rise on her flesh. 'What exactly do you think you know about me?'

'Sex is your weapon of choice.'

'I beg your pardon?' she squeaked as the backs of her legs touched the side of the bed. 'Did you just say—?'

'You need to learn to finesse your art, though. No man likes to be bludgeoned over the head with sex. No matter how…enticing the package.'

'You're either loopy or you've got me confused with someone else. I don't bludgeon and I don't entice.'

He kept coming. She leaned back on the bed and felt the hem of her shirt riding up her thighs.

'For goodness' sake, stop!'

He stopped, but his gaze didn't. It continued its destructive course over her, leaving no part of her untouched, until Sasha felt sure she was about to combust from the heat of it.

Desperate, she darted out her tongue to lick her lips. 'Look, I'm not who…whatever you think I am.'

'Even though I can see the evidence for myself?' he rasped in a low voice.

Maya Blake fell in love with the world of the alpha male and the strong, aspirational heroine when she borrowed her sister's Mills & Boon® at age thirteen. Shortly thereafter the dream to plot a happy ending for her own characters was born. Writing for Harlequin Mills & Boon is a dream come true. Maya lives in South East England with her husband and two kids. Reading is an absolute passion, but when she isn't lost in a book she likes to swim, cycle, travel and Tweet!

You can get in touch with her via e-mail, at mayablake@ymail.com, or on Twitter: www.twitter.com/mayablake

THE PRICE OF SUCCESS
is Maya's debut book
for Mills & Boon® Modern™ Romance!

THE PRICE
OF SUCCESS

BY
MAYA BLAKE

First published in Great Britain 2012
by Mills & Boon, an imprint of Harlequin (UK) Limited.
Harlequin (UK) Limited, Eton House, 18-24 Paradise Road,
Richmond, Surrey TW9 1SR

© Maya Blake 2012

ISBN: 978 0 263 22844 1

THE PRICE
OF SUCCESS

First and foremost for my dear sister, Barbara, who gave me the book that started this wonderful journey. For my husband, Tony, for his unwavering support and firm belief that this dream would become reality. For my HEART sisters—your incredible support kept me going right from the beginning—thank you! And finally for my darling MINXES! You are the best cheerleaders a girl can have and I'd be totally lost without you.

CHAPTER ONE

THE moments before the crash played out almost in slow motion. Time paused, then stretched lethargically in the Sunday sun. And even though the cars were travelling at over two hundred and twenty kilometers an hour, there seemed an almost hypnotic, ballet-like symmetry in their movement.

Sasha Fleming stared, frozen, her heart suspended mid-beat, terrified to complete its task as Rafael's front wing clipped the rear tyre of the slower back marker. Hundreds of thousands of pounds' worth of carbon fibre bent backwards, twisted in on itself. Ripped metal tore through the left tyre, wrenching the car into a ninety-degree turn.

The world-renowned racing car launched itself into the air. For several brief seconds it looked more like a futuristic aircraft than an asphalt-hugging machine.

Inevitably, gravity won out. The explosion was deafening as sound erupted all around her. The screech of contorting metal rang through her head, amplified by the super-sized loudspeakers all around her. In the next instant the white concrete wall just after the Turn One hairpin bend was streaked with the iconic racing green paint of Rafael's car.

'He's crashed! He's crashed! The pole sitter and current world champion, Rafael de Cervantes, has crashed his Espiritu DSII. Only this morning the papers said this car was uncrashable. How wrong were they?'

Sasha ripped off her headphones, unable to stomach the frenzied glee in the commentator's voice or the huge roar that rose around the Hungaroring circuit.

Her heart, now making up for its sluggishness, was beating so hard and so fast it threatened to break through her ribcage. Her eyes remained glued to the bank of screens on the pit wall, and she and two dozen pit crew members watched the horrific events unfold.

'Turn up the sound,' someone yelled.

Curbing a wild need to negate that command, she clamped her lips together, arms folded tight around her middle. Memories of another time, another crash, played alongside the carnage unfolding on the screen. Unable to stem it, she let the memories of the event that had changed her for ever filter through to play alongside this appalling spectacle.

'Sometimes the only way to get through pain is to immerse yourself in it. Let it eat you alive. It'll spit you out eventually.'

How many times had her father told her that? When she'd broken her ankle learning to ride her bike. When she'd fractured her arm falling out of a tree. When she'd lost her mum when she was ten. When she'd suffered the desperate consequences of falling for the wrong guy.

She'd got through them all. Well…almost.

The secret loss she'd buried deep in her heart would always be with her. As would the loss of her father.

The commentator's voice scythed through her thoughts. *'There's no movement from the car. The race has been red-flagged and the safety car is on its way. So is the ambulance. But so far we haven't seen Rafael move. His engineer will be frantically trying to speak to him, no doubt. I must say, though, it's not looking good…'*

Sasha forced in a breath, her fingers moving convulsively to loosen the Velcro securing her constricting race suit. A shudder raked her frame, followed closely by another. She tried to swallow but she couldn't get her throat to work.

Alongside the thoughts zipping through her head, her last conversation with Rafael filtered through.

He'd been so angry with her. And the accusations he'd flung at her when she'd only been trying to help...

Ice clutched her soul. Was this *her* fault? Had *she* played a part in this carnage?

'*The ambulance is there now. And there's Rafael's brother, Marco, the owner of Team Espiritu. He's on his way to the crash site...hopefully we'll get a progress report soon.*'

Marco. Another fist of shock punched through her flailing senses. She hadn't even been aware he'd finally arrived in Hungary. In her two years as reserve driver for Team Espiritu, Marco de Cervantes hadn't missed a single race—until this weekend.

The whole paddock had been abuzz with his absence, the celebrities and royalty who jetted in from all over the world specifically to experience the de Cervantes lifestyle, visibly disappointed. From Rafael's terse response when she'd asked of his brother's whereabouts, Sasha had concluded the brothers had fallen out.

Her heart twisted tighter in her chest at the thought that Marco had finally arrived only to witness his brother's crash.

A daring cameraman broke through the flanking bodyguards and caught up with Marco. Tight-jawed, his olive skin showing only the barest hint of paleness, he kept his gaze fixed ahead, his set expression not revealing the slightest hint of his emotional state as he strode towards the courtesy car waiting a few feet away.

Just before he got into the car he turned his head. Deep hazel eyes stared straight into the camera.

Sasha's breath stilled. Icy dread flooded her veins at the banked fury in their depths. His features were pinched, his mouth a taut line, the lines bracketing his mouth deep and austere. Everything about him indicated he was reining in tight emotion. Not surprising, given the circumstances.

But, eerily, Sasha knew his emotion extended beyond the events unfolding now. Whatever emotion Marco was holding in, it went far beyond his reaction to his brother's horrific accident.

Another shiver raked through her. She turned away from the

screen, searching blindly for an escape. The back of the garage where the tyres were stacked offered a temporary sanctuary.

She'd taken one single step towards the opening when her heart sank. Tom Brooks, her personal press officer, broke away from the crew and made a beeline for her.

'We need to prep for an interview,' he clipped out, fingers flying over his iPad.

Nausea rose to join all the other sensations percolating inside her. 'Already? We don't even know how Rafael is.' Or even if he was still alive.

'Exactly. The eyes of the world will be on this team. Now's not the time to bungle our way through another disastrous soundbite,' he said unsympathetically.

Sasha bit her lip. Her heated denial of a relationship with Rafael only a week ago had fuelled media speculation, and brought unwanted focus on the team.

'Surely it's better to be well informed before the interview than to go on air half-cocked?'

His face darkened. 'Do you want to be a reserve driver for ever?'

Sasha frowned. 'Of course not—'

'Good, because I don't want to play press officer to a reserve driver for the rest of my career. You want to be one of the boys? Here's your chance to prove it.'

A wave of anger rose inside her. 'I don't need to be heartless to prove myself, Tom.'

'Oh, but you do. Do you think any of the other drivers would hesitate at the chance that's been presented?'

'What chance? We don't even know how Rafael is doing yet!'

'Well, you can sit on your hands until the moment's snatched from you. The handful of female X1 Premier Racing drivers who've gone before you barely made an impact. You can choose to become a meaningless statistic, or you can put yourself in the driver's seat—literally—and lay the paddock rumours to rest.'

She didn't need to ask what he meant. A wave of pain rolled through her. Pushing it back, she straightened her shoulders. 'I don't care about rumours. I'm a good driver—'

'You're also Jack Fleming's daughter and Derek Mahoney's ex. If you want to be taken seriously you need to step out of their shadows. Do the interview. Stake your claim.'

As his fingers resumed their busy course over his iPad, unease rose inside Sasha. As much as she disliked Tom's acerbic attitude, a part of her knew he was right. The move from reserve to full-time driver for Team Espiritu was a once-in-a-lifetime opportunity she couldn't afford to squander—not if she wanted to achieve her goals.

'I have a reporter ready to meet—'

'No.' Her gaze flicked to the screen and her resolve strengthened. 'I won't give an interview until I hear how Rafael is.'

Two ambulances and three fire engines now surrounded the mangled car. Sparks flew as the fire crew cut away the chassis.

Marco de Cervantes stood scant feet away, ignoring everyone, his impressive physique firmly planted, hands balled into fists, his unwavering gaze fixed on his brother's still form. Sasha's heart squeezed tighter.

Please be alive, Rafael. Don't you dare die on me...

Tom's stern look mellowed slightly as he followed her gaze. 'I'll prepare something while we wait. Find a quiet place. Get yourself together.' He glanced around, made sure he wasn't overheard and leaned in closer. 'This is the chance you've been waiting for, Sasha. *Don't blow it.*'

Marco de Cervantes stepped into the private hospital room in Budapest, sick dread churning through his stomach. He clenched his fists to stop the shaking in his hands and forced himself to walk to his brother's bedside. With each step the accident replayed in his mind's eye, a vivid, gruesome nightmare that wouldn't stop. There'd been so much blood at the crash site... *so much blood...*

His chest tightened as he saw the white sheet pulled over his brother's chest.

Absently, he made a note to have the staff replace the sheets with another colour—green, perhaps, Rafael's favourite colour. White hospital sheets looked...smelled...too much like death.

Rafael wasn't dead. And if Marco had anything to do with it this would be his last senseless brush with death. Enough was enough.

He drew level with the bed and stared down into his brother's pale, still face. At the tube inserted into his mouth to help him breathe.

Enough was enough.

Marco's throat closed up. He'd chosen to give Rafael time to come to his senses instead of forcing him to listen to reason. And by doing so he'd allowed his brother to take the wheel behind the world's most powerful car while still reeling from emotional rejection.

Unlike him, his brother had never been able to compartmentalise his life, to suppress superfluous emotions that led to unnecessarily clouded judgement. Rafael coalesced happiness, sadness, triumph and loss into one hot, sticky mess. Add the lethal mix of a seven hundred and fifty horsepower racing car, and once again *he* was left picking up the pieces.

His breath shuddered. Reaching out, he took Rafael's unmoving hand, leaned down until his lips hovered an inch from his brother's ear.

'You live—you hear me? I swear on all things holy, if you die on me I'll track you to hell and kick your ass,' he grated out, then swallowed the thickness in his throat. 'And I know you'll be in hell, because you sure as heck won't get into heaven with *those* looks.'

His voice caught and he forced back his tears.

Rafael's hand remained immobile, barely warm. Marco held on tighter, desperately infusing his brother with his own life force, desperately trying to block out the doctor's words...*his brain is swelling...there's internal bleeding...nothing to do but wait...*

With a stifled curse, he whirled away from the bed. The window of the ultra-private, ultra-exclusive, state-of-the-art hospital looked out onto a serene courtyard, with discreet fountains and carefully clipped flowers meant to soothe the troubled patient. Beyond the grounds, forests stretched as far as the eye could see.

Marco found no solace in the picturesque view. He found even less to smile about when his eyes lit on the paparazzi waiting beyond the hospital's boundaries, powerful lenses trained, ready to pounce.

Shoving a hand through his hair, he turned back to the bed.

A flash of green caught the corner of his eye. He focused on the flat-screen TV mounted on the wall and watched Rafael's accident replayed again in slow motion.

Bile rose to his throat. Reaching blindly for the remote, he aimed it at the screen—only to stop when another picture shifted into focus.

Anger escalated through him. Five minutes later he stabbed the 'off' button and calmly replaced the control.

Returning to Rafael's bedside, his sank onto the side of the bed. 'I know you'd probably argue with me, *mi hermano*, but you've had a lucky escape. In more ways than one.'

Jaw clenching, he thanked heaven his brother hadn't heard the interview just played on TV. Marco had first-hand knowledge of what people would sacrifice in their quest for fame and power, and the look of naked ambition in Sasha Fleming's eyes made his chest burn with fury and his skin crawl.

His fist tightened on the bed next to his brother's unmoving body.

If she wanted a taste of power he would give it to her. Let her acquire a taste for it the way she'd given Rafael a taste of herself.

Then, just as she'd callously shoved Rafael aside, Marco would take utter satisfaction in wrenching away everything she'd ever dreamed of.

'Excuse me, can you tell me which room Rafael de Cervantes is in?' Sasha infused her voice with as much authority as possible, despite the glaring knowledge that she wasn't supposed to be here.

The nurse dressed in a crisp white uniform looked up. The crease already forming on her brow caused Sasha's heart to sink.

'Are you a member of the family?'

'No, but I wanted to see how he was. He was...*is* my team

mate.' The moment the words left her lips she winced. *Way to go, Sasha.*

True to form, the nurse's frown dissolved as realisation dawned. 'His team mate...? You're Sasha Fleming!'

Sasha summoned her practised camera smile—the one that held the right amount of interest without screaming *look at me*, and lifted the oversized sunglasses. 'Yes,' she murmured.

'My nephew *loves* you!' The nurse gushed. 'He pretends not to, but I know he thinks you rock. Every time he sees you during Friday Practice his face lights up. He'll be thrilled when I tell him I met you.'

The tension clamping Sasha's nape eased a little. 'Thanks. So can I see Rafael?' she asked again. When the frown threatened to make a comeback, Sasha rushed on. 'I'll only be a moment, I promise.'

'I'm sorry, Miss Fleming. You're not on my list of approved visitors.'

Steeling herself against the nerves dragging through her, Sasha cleared her throat. 'Is Marco de Cervantes here? Maybe I can ask him?'

She pushed the mental picture of Marco's cold, unforgiving features to the back of her mind. She was here for Rafael. Surely, as his team mate, his brother wouldn't bar her from seeing him?

'No, he left half an hour ago.'

Shock slammed into her. 'He *left*?'

The nurse nodded. 'He didn't seem too happy, but considering the circumstances I guess it's to be expected.'

For a moment Sasha debated asking if the nurse would make an exception. Break the rules for her. But she dismissed it. Breaking her own rules, getting friendly with Rafael, was probably the reason he'd ended up in this situation. She refused to exacerbate it.

Plucking her sunglasses off her head, she slid them down to cover her eyes. In her jeans and long-sleeved cotton top, with a multi-coloured cheesecloth satchel slung across her body, she looked like every other summer tourist in the city. Her disguise had helped her evade the paparazzi on her way in. She prayed it would hold up on her way out.

With a heavy heart she turned towards the elevator doors, which stood open as if to usher her away from here as fast as possible.

'Wait.' The nurse beckoned with a quick hand movement and leaned forward as Sasha approached the desk. 'Maybe I can sneak you in for a few minutes,' she whispered.

Relief washed over Sasha. 'Oh, thank you so much!'

'If you don't mind signing an autograph for my nephew?'

A tinge of guilt arrowed through her, but the need to see Rafael overcame the feeling. With a grateful smile, Sasha took the proffered pen.

'What the hell are you doing in here?'

Sasha spun round at the harsh voice, and gasped at the dark figure framed in the doorway. A few minutes, the nurse had said. A quick glance at her watch confirmed her sickening suspicion. She'd been here almost an hour!

'I asked you a question.'

'I came to see Rafael. There was no one here—'

'So you thought you'd just sneak in?'

'Hardly! The nurse—' Sasha gulped back her words, realising she could be putting the nurse's job in jeopardy.

'The nurse what?'

Marco advanced into the room, his formidable presence shrinking the space. She scrambled to her feet, but she still had to tilt her head to see his face.

His cold-as-steel expression dried her mouth further.

She shook her head. 'I just wanted to see how he was.' She stopped speaking as he drew level with her, his hard eyes boring into her.

'How long have you been here?'

She risked another glance at her watch and cringed inwardly. Dared she tell him the truth or blag her way through? 'Does it really matter?'

'How long?' he gritted, his gaze sliding over his brother as if assessing any further damage.

'Why are you checking him over like that? Do you think I've harmed him in some way?' she challenged.

Hazel eyes slammed back to her. His contempt was evident as his gaze raked her face. 'I don't *think*! I *know* you've already harmed my brother.'

His tone was so scathing Sasha was surprised her flesh wasn't falling from her skin.

'Rafael told you about our fight?'

'Yes, he did. I can only conclude that your presence here is another media stunt, not out of concern for my brother?'

'Of course it isn't!'

'Is that why the media presence at the hospital gates has doubled in the last hour?'

Her gaze drifted to the window. The blinds were drawn against the late-afternoon sun, but not closed completely. She'd taken a step to look for herself when steely fingers closed on her wrist. Heat shot up her arm, the reaction so unfamiliar she froze.

'If you think I'm going to let you use my brother to further your own ends, you're sorely mistaken.'

Alarmed, she stared up at him. 'Why would you think I'd do that?'

A mirthless smile bared his teeth, displaying a look so frightening she shivered.

'That press conference you gave? About how much you cared for him? How your thoughts were with him and his family? *About how you're willing to step into his shoes as soon as possible so you don't let the team down?* What were your exact words? *"I've earned the chance at a full-time seat. I've proven that I have what it takes."'*

Sasha swallowed, unable to look away from the chilling but oddly hypnotic pull of his gaze. 'I...I shouldn't have....' The echo of unease she'd felt before and during the interview returned. 'I didn't mean it like that—'

'How *did* you mean it, then? How exactly have *you*, a mere reserve driver, earned your place on the team? Why do *you* deserve Rafael's seat and not one of the other dozen top drivers out there?'

'Because it's my time! I deserve the chance.' She wrenched at her captured arm. His hand tightened, sending another bolt of heat through her body.

Straight black brows clamped together. His arresting features were seriously eroding her thought processes. Even livid to the point where she could imagine heat striations coming off his body he oozed enough sex appeal to make her finally understand why his bodyguards were forever turning away paddock groupies from his luxury hospitality suite. Rumour had it that one particularly eager groupie had scaled the mobile suite and slipped into his bedroom via the skylight.

'*Your time?* Why?' he challenged again, stepping closer, invading her body space and her ability to breathe. 'What's so special about *you*, Sasha Fleming?'

'I didn't say I was special.'

'That's not what I got from the press junket. In fact I deduced something along the lines that the team would be making a huge mistake if you weren't given Rafael's seat. Was there even the veiled threat of a lawsuit thrown in there?'

The thought that this might be her only chance to find a decent seat had resonated in the back of her mind even as she'd felt sickened at the thought of how wrong the timing was.

'Nothing to say?' came the soft taunt.

She finally managed to wrench her wrist from his grasp and stepped back. 'Mr de Cervantes, this is neither the time nor the place to discuss this.'

Her glance slid to Rafael, her throat closing in distress at the tubes and the horrid beeping of the machines keeping him alive.

Marco followed her gaze and froze, as if just realising where he was. When his gaze sliced back to hers she glimpsed a well of anguish within the hazel depths and felt something soften inside her. Marco de Cervantes, despite his chilling words and seriously imposing presence, was hurting. The fear of the unknown, of wondering if the precious life of someone you held dear would pull through was one she was agonisingly familiar with.

Any thought of her job flew out of her head as she watched him wrestle with his pain. The urge to comfort, one human being to another, momentarily overcame her instinct for self-preservation.

'Rafael is strong. He's a fighter. He'll pull through,' she murmured softly.

Slowly he pulled in a breath, and any hint of pain disappeared. His upper lip curled in a mocking sneer. 'Your concern is touching, Miss Fleming. But cut the crap. There are no cameras here. No microphones to lap up your false platitudes. Unless you've got one hidden on your person?' His eyes slid down her body, narrowing as they searched. 'Will I go on the internet tomorrow and see footage of my brother in his sick bed all over it?'

'That's a tasteless and disgusting thing to say!' Spinning away, she rushed to the leather sofa in the suite and picked up her satchel. Clearly it was time to make herself scarce.

Careful not to come within touching distance of Marco de Cervantes, she edged towards the door.

'Any more tasteless than you vying for his seat even before you knew for certain whether he was alive or dead?' came the biting query.

Sasha winced. 'I agree. It wasn't the perfect time to do an interview.'

A hint of surprise lightened his eyes, but his lips firmed a second later. 'But you did it anyway.'

Blaming Tom would have been easy. And the coward's way out. The truth was, she *wanted* to be lead driver.

'I thought I was acting in the best interests of the team. And, yes, I was also putting myself forward as the most viable option. But the timing was wrong. For that, I apologise.'

That grim smile made another appearance. Her body shuddered with alarm. Even before he spoke Sasha had the strongest premonition that she wasn't going to like the words that spilled from his lips.

'You should've taken more time to think, Miss Fleming. Because, as team owner, *I* ultimately decide what's in the best interests of Team Espiritu. Not you.'

He sauntered to his brother's bedside and stood looking down at him.

Sasha glanced between the two men. This close, the resemblance between them was striking. Yet they couldn't have been more different. Where Rafael was wild and gregarious, his brother smouldered and rumbled like the deepest, darkest underbelly of a dormant volcano. The fear that he could erupt at any moment was a very real and credible threat. One that made her throat dry and her heart race.

Finally he turned to face her. Trepidation iced its way to her toes.

'My decision and mine alone carries. Your timing wasn't just wrong. It was detestable.' His voice could have frozen water in the Sahara. 'It also makes my decision incredibly easy.'

Her heart stopped. 'Wh—what decision?'

'Relieving you of your job, of course.' The smile widened. 'Congratulations. You're fired.'

CHAPTER TWO

'WHAT?'

'Get out.'

Sasha remained frozen, unable to heed Marco de Cervantes's command. Finally she forced out a breath.

'No. You—you can't do that. You can't fire me.' Somewhere at the back of her mind she knew this to be true—something about contracts…clauses—but her brain couldn't seem to track after the blow it had been dealt.

'I can do anything I want. I *own* the team. Which means I own you.'

'Yes, but…' She sucked in a breath and forced herself to focus. 'Yes, you own the team, but you don't *own* me. And you can't fire me. I haven't done anything wrong. Sure, the press interview was a little mistimed. But that isn't grounds to sack me.'

'Maybe those aren't the only grounds I have.'

Cold dread eased up her spine. 'What are you talking about?'

Marco regarded her for several seconds. Then his gaze slid to his brother. Reaching out, he carefully smoothed back a lock of hair from Rafael's face. The poignancy of the gesture and the momentary softening of his features made Sasha's heart ache for him, despite his anger at her. No one deserved to watch a loved one suffer. Not even Marco de Cervantes.

When his gaze locked onto her again Sasha wasn't prepared for the mercurial shift from familial concern to dark fury.

'You're right. My brother's bedside isn't the place to discuss this.' He came towards her, his long-legged stride purposeful and arrestingly graceful. His broad shoulders, the strength in his lean, muscled body demanded an audience. Sasha stared, unable to look away from the perfect body packed full of angry Spanish male.

In whose path she directly stood.

At the last second her legs unfroze long enough for her to step out of his way. 'It's okay. I'll leave.'

'Running away? Scared your past is catching up with you, Miss Fleming?'

She swallowed carefully, striving to maintain a neutral expression. Marco de Cervantes didn't know. He *couldn't*.

'I don't know what you're talking about. My past has nothing to do with my contract with your team.'

He stared into her face for so long Sasha wanted to slam on the shades dangling uselessly from her fingers.

'Extraordinary,' he finally murmured.

'What?' she croaked.

'You lie so flawlessly. Not even an eyelash betrays you. It's no wonder Rafael was completely taken with you. What I don't understand is why. He offered you what you wanted—money, prestige, a privileged lifestyle millions dream about but only few achieve. Isn't that what women like you ultimately want? The chance to live in unimaginable luxury playing mistress of a *castillo*?'

'Um, I don't know what sort of women *you've* been cavorting with, but you know nothing about me.'

Impossibly, his features grew colder. 'I know everything I need to know. So why didn't you just take it? What's your angle?' His intense gaze bored into her, as if trying to burrow beneath her skin.

It took every control-gathering technique she'd learned not to step back from him.

'I have no *angle*—'

'Enough of your lies. Get out.' He wrenched the door open, fully expecting her to comply.

Her eyes flicked to Rafael's still form. Sasha doubted she'd see him again before the team's month-long August break. 'Will you tell him I came to see him when he wakes up—please?' she asked.

Marco exhaled in disbelief. 'With any luck, by the time my brother wakes up any memory he has of you will be wiped clean from his mind.'

She gasped, the chill from his voice washing over her. 'I'm not sure exactly what Rafael told you, but you've really got this wrong.'

Marco shrugged. 'And you're still fired. Goodbye, Miss Fleming.'

'On what grounds?' she challenged, hoping this time her voice would emerge with more conviction.

'I'm sure my lawyers can find something. Inappropriate enthusiasm?'

'That's a reason you should be keeping me on—not a reason to fire me.'

'You've just proved my point. Most people know where to draw the line. It seems you don't.'

'I *do*,' she stressed, her voice rising right along with the tight knot in her chest.

'This conversation is over.' He glanced pointedly at the door.

She stepped into the corridor, reeling from the impact of his words. Her contract was airtight. She was sure of it. But she'd seen too many teams discard perfectly fit and able drivers for reasons far flimsier than the one Marco had just given her. X1 Premier Racing was notorious for its court battles between team owners and drivers.

The thought that she could lose everything she'd fought for made her mouth dry. She'd battled hard to hold onto her seat in the most successful team in the history of the sport, when every punter with a blog or a social media account had taken potshots at her talent. One particularly harsh critic had even gone as far as to debate her sexual preferences.

She'd sacrificed too much for too long. Somehow she had to convince Marco de Cervantes to keep her on.

She turned to confront him—only to find a short man wearing a suit and a fawning expression hurrying towards them. He handed Marco a small wooden box and launched into a rapid volley of French. Whatever the man—whose discreet badge announced him as Administrator—was saying, it wasn't having any effect on Marco.

Marco's response was clipped. When the administrator started in surprise and glanced towards the reception area, Sasha followed his gaze. The nurse who had let her in stood behind the counter.

The administrator launched into another obsequious torrent. Marco cut him off with an incisive slash of his hand and headed for the lifts.

Sasha hurried after him. As she passed the reception area, she glimpsed the naked distress in the nurse's eyes. Another wave of icy dread slammed into her, lending her more impetus as she rushed after Marco.

'Wait!'

He pressed the button for the lift as she screeched to a halt beside him.

Away from the low lights of the hospital room Sasha saw him—really saw him—for the first time. Up close and personal, Marco de Cervantes was stunning. If you liked your men tall, imposing and bristling with tons of masculinity. Through the gap in his grey cotton shirt she caught a glimpse of dark hair and a strong, golden chest that had her glancing away in a hurry.

Focus!

'Can we talk—please?' she injected into the silence.

He ignored her, his stern, closed face forbidding any conversation. The lift arrived and he stepped in. Sasha rushed in after him. As the doors closed she saw the nurse burst into tears.

Outraged, she rounded on him. 'My God. You got that nurse sacked, didn't you?'

Anger dissolved the last of her instinctive self-preservation and washed away the strangely compelling sensation she refused to acknowledge was attraction.

'I lodged a complaint.'

'Which, coming from you, was as good as ordering that administrator to sack her!'

Guilt attacked her insides.

'She must live with the consequences of her actions.'

'So there's no in-between? No showing mercy? Just straight to the gallows?'

Deep hazel eyes pinned her where she stood. 'You weren't on the list of approved visitors. She knew this and disregarded it. You could've been a tabloid hack. Anybody.'

His eyes narrowed and Sasha forced her expression to remain neutral.

'Or maybe she knew *exactly* who you were?'

She lowered her lids as a wave of guilty heat washed over her face.

'Of course,' he taunted softly. 'What did you offer her? Free tickets to the next race?'

Deciding silence was the best policy, she clamped her lips together.

'A personal tour of the paddock and a photo op with you once you became lead driver, perhaps?'

His scathing tone grated on her nerves.

Raising her head she met his gaze, anger at his high-handedness loosening her tongue. 'You know, just because your brother is gravely ill, it doesn't give you the right to destroy other people's lives.'

'I beg your pardon?' he bit out.

'Right now you're in pain and lashing out, wanting anyone and everyone to pay for what you're going through. It's understandable, but it's not fair. That poor woman is now jobless just because *you're* angry.'

'*That poor woman* abused her position and broke the hospital's policy for personal gain. She deserves everything she gets.'

'It wasn't for personal gain. She did it for her nephew. He's a fan. She wanted to do something nice for him.'

'My heart bleeds.'

'You do the same, and more, for thousands of race fans every year. What's so different about this?'

Dark brows clamped together, and his jaw tightened in that barely civilised way that sent another wave of apprehension through her. Again she glimpsed the dark fury riding just below his outward control.

'The difference, Miss Fleming, is that I don't compromise my integrity to do so. And I don't put those I care about in harm's way just to get what I want.'

'What about compassion?'

His brows cleared, but the volatile tinge in the air remained. 'I'm fresh out.'

'You know, you'll wake up one morning not long from now and regret your actions today.'

The lift doors glided open to reveal the underground car park. A few feet away was a gleaming black chrome-trimmed Bentley Continental. Beside it, a driver and a heavily muscled man whose presence shrieked *bodyguard* waited. The driver held the back door open, but Marco made no move towards it. Instead he glanced down at her, his expression hauntingly bleak.

'I regret a lot that's happened in the past twenty-four hours—not least watching my brother mangle himself and his car on the race track because he believed himself to be heartbroken. One more thing doesn't make a difference.'

'Your emotions are overwhelming you right now. All I'm saying is don't let them overrule your better judgement.'

A cold smile lifted one corner of his mouth. 'My *emotions*? I didn't know you practised on the side as the team's psychologist. I thought you'd ridden down with me to beg for your job back, not to practise the elevator pitch version of pop psychology. You had me as your captive audience for a full thirty seconds. Shame you chose to waste it.'

'Mock me all you want. It doesn't change the fact that you're acting like—' She bit her lip, common sense momentarily overriding her anger.

'Go on,' he encouraged softly. Tauntingly. 'Acting like what?'

She shrugged. 'Like…well, like an ass.'

His eyes narrowed until they were mere icy slits. 'Excuse me?'

'Sorry. You asked.'

Anger flared in his eyes, radiated off his body. Sasha held

her breath, readying herself for the explosion about to rain on her head. Instead he gave a grim smile.

'I've been called worse.' He nodded to his bodyguard, who took a step towards them. 'Romano will escort you off the premises. Be warned—my very generous donation to this hospital is contingent on you being arrested if you set foot anywhere near my brother again. I'm sure the administrator would relish that challenge.'

Despair rose to mingle with her anger. 'You can't do this. If you don't listen to me I'll…I'll talk to the press again. I'll spill everything!'

'Ah, I'm glad to finally meet the *real* you, Miss Fleming.'

'Ten minutes. That's all I want. Let me convince you to keep me on.'

'Trust me—blackmail isn't a great place to start.'

She bit her lip. 'That was just a bluff. I won't talk to the press. But I do want to drive for you. And I'm the best mid-season replacement you'll find for Rafael.'

'You *do* place a high premium on yourself, don't you?'

Unflinching, she nodded. 'Yes, I do. And I can back it up. Just let me prove it.'

His gaze narrowed on her face, then conducted a lazy sweep over her body. Suddenly the clothes that had served as perfect camouflage against the intrusive press felt inadequate, exposing. Beneath the thin material of her T-shirt her heart hammered, her skin tingling with an alien awareness that made her muscles tense.

As a female driver in a predominantly male sport, she was used to being the cynosure of male eyes. There were those who searched for signs of failure as a driver, ready to use any shortcomings against her. Then there were the predators who searched for weaknesses simply because she was a woman, and therefore deemed incapable. The most vicious lot were those who bided their time, ready to rip her apart because she was Jack Fleming's daughter. Those were the ones she feared the most. And the ones she'd sworn to prove wrong.

Marco de Cervantes's gaze held an intensity that combined

all of those qualities multiplied by a thousand. And then there was something else.

Something that made her breath grow shallow in her lungs. Made her palms clammy and the hairs bristle on her nape.

Recalling the sheer intensity of the look he'd directed into the camera earlier, she felt her heartbeat accelerate.

'Get in the car,' he bit out, his tone bone-chilling.

Sasha glanced into the dark, luxurious interior of the limo and hesitated. The feelings this man engendered in her weren't those of fear. Rather, she sensed an emotional risk—as if, given half a chance, he would burrow under her skin, discover her worst fears and use them against her. She couldn't let that happen.

'If you want me to hear you out you'll get in the car. Now,' he said, his tone uncompromising.

She hesitated. 'I can't.'

'*Can't* isn't a word I enjoy hearing,' he growled, his patience clearly ebbing fast.

'My bike.' He quirked one brow at her. 'I'd *rather* not leave it here.'

His glance towards the battered green and white scooter leaning precariously against the car park wall held disbelief. 'You came here on *that*?'

'Yes. Why?'

'You're wearing the most revolting pair of jeans I've ever seen and a scarf that's seen better days. Add that to the oversized sunglasses and I don't need to be a genius to guess you were trying some misguided attempt to escape the paparazzi. I am right?' At her nod, he continued. 'And yet you travelled on the slowest mode of motorised transport known to man.'

She raised her chin. 'But there's the beauty—don't you see? I managed to ride straight past the paparazzi without one single camera lens focusing on me. You, on the other hand... Tell me— how did they react when you rocked up in your huge, tinted-windowed monstrosity of a car?'

His jaw tightened and he glared at her.

'Exactly. I'm not leaving my bike.'

'Security here is—'

'Inadequate, according to you. After all, *I* managed to get through, didn't I?' She threw his words back at him.

One hand gripped the door of the car. 'Get in the car or don't. I refuse to argue with you over a pile of junk.'

'It's my junk and I won't leave it.'

With a stifled curse, Marco held out his hands. 'Keys?'

'Why?'

'Romano will return the scooter to your hotel.'

Sasha's eyes widened. Romano weighed at least two hundred and fifty pounds of pure muscle. The thought of what he'd put her poor scooter through made her wince.

'And before you comment on Romano's size I'd urge you to stop and think about his *feelings*,' Marco added mockingly.

Touché, she conceded silently.

Digging into her satchel, she reluctantly handed over her keys. Marco lobbed them to his bodyguard, then raised an imperious eyebrow at her.

With a resigned sigh, Sasha slid past his imposing body and entered the limo.

The door shut on them, enclosing them in a silent cocoon that threatened to send her already taut nerves into a frenzied tailspin.

As the car glided out of the car park it occurred to her that she had no idea where Marco was taking her. She opened her mouth to ask, then immediately shut it when she saw his gaze fixed on the small box.

Despite his bleak expression, his profile was stunningly arresting. The sculpted contours of his face held enough shadow and intrigue to capture the attention of any red-blooded female with a pulse—a fact attested to by the regular parade of stunning women he was photographed with.

His strong jaw bore the beginnings of a five o'clock shadow, and an even stronger, taut neck slanted onto impossibly broad shoulders. Under the discreetly expensive cotton shirt those shoulders moved restlessly. She followed the movement, her gaze sliding down over his chest, past the flat stomach that showed no hint of flab. Her eyes rested in his lap. The bulge beneath his zipper made heat swirl in her belly.

'Have you seen enough? Or would you like me to perform a slow striptease for you?'

Her cheeks burned. Her neck burned. In fact for several seconds Sasha was sure her whole body was on fire. Mortified, she hastily plucked her sunglasses from atop her head and jammed them onto her face.

'I… You didn't say where we were going.'

'I've called a meeting with Russell and the chief engineer. I'm handing over the reins temporarily so I can concentrate on making arrangements for Rafael to be evacuated home to Spain.'

'You're moving him?'

'Not yet, but the medical team is on standby. He'll be moved the moment it's deemed safe.'

'I see.'

Sharp eyes bored into her. 'Do you? You've talked your way into a last-chance meeting and yet you're wasting time exhibiting false concern for my brother.'

She sucked in a breath. 'My concern isn't false. I'd give anything for Rafael not to be in that place.'

Sasha watched, fascinated, as his hand tightened around the box. 'In my experience *anything* tends to arrive with a very heavy price tag and a carefully calculated catch. So be very careful with your choice of words.'

Sasha licked her lips, suddenly unable to breathe at the expression in his eyes. 'I'm sure I don't know what you mean.'

The look in his eyes hardened. 'You really should try a different profession. Your acting skills are highly commendable.'

'Driving suits me just fine, thanks. Where are we going, exactly?'

Keeping his gaze on her, he relaxed back in his seat. 'My hotel.'

'Your hotel?' she repeated dully. Her senses, still reeling after she'd been caught staring at Marco de Cervantes's man package, threatened to go into freefall. The thought of being alone with him—truly alone—made anxiety skitter over her skin. 'I don't think that's a good idea.'

'You don't have a choice. You wanted this meeting.'

Desperation lent her voice strength. 'The rest of the team will be wondering where I am. Maybe I should let them know.' Tom had asked where she was going after the press conference, but she'd been deliberately evasive.

'The team will be out doing what they do after every Sunday race. Bar hopping and trying it on with the local girls.'

'I don't think they'll be doing that tonight. Not with Rafael...' She bit her lip, unable to continue as she glimpsed the flash of pain in those hazel eyes.

But he merely shrugged. 'Call them if you want. Tell them where you're going. And why.'

Not expecting her bluff to be called, Sasha floundered. The circumstances of her past made it impossible to make friends with anyone on her team. The constant whispers behind her back, the conversations that stopped when she walked into a room, made it hard to trust anyone.

Tom only cared as far as her actions impacted upon his career. The only one who had cared—really cared—had been Rafael. A wave of pain and regret rushed through her. Until their row last night she'd foolishly let herself believe she could finally trust another human being.

Feigning nonchalance, she shrugged. 'I'll tell them later.'

Unable to stomach the mockery in Marco's eyes, she turned away.

Absently she stroked the armrest, silently apologising for calling the Bentley Continental a monstrosity. Amongst the luxury, sometimes vacuous, creations car manufacturers produced, the Bentley was one of the more ingenious styles. It had been her father's favourite non-racing car—his pride and joy until he'd been forced to sell it to defend himself.

'We're here.'

They were parked beneath the pillared portico of the Four Seasons. A liveried doorman stepped forward and opened the door on Marco's side, his bow of deference deep to the point of being obsequious.

Casting her gaze past him, Sasha felt her mouth drop open at the sheer opulence of the marbled foyer of the stunning hotel. The whole atmosphere glittered and sparkled beneath a super-sized revolving chandelier, which was throwing its adoring light on sleekly dressed patrons.

Sasha remained in her seat, super-conscious of how inappropriate her old hipster jeans and worn top were for the gold-leaf and five-star luxury spread before her. She was pretty sure she would be directed to the tradesman's entrance the moment the doorman saw her scuffed boots.

'Come out. And lose the glasses and the scarf. No one cares who you are here.'

She hesitated. 'Can't we just talk in the car?' she ventured.

He held out a commanding hand. 'No, we can't. We both know you're not shy, so stop wasting my time.'

She could argue, defend her personal reputation against the label Marco had decided to pin on her, but Sasha doubted it would make a difference. He, like the rest of the world, believed she was soiled goods because of her past and because she was a Fleming.

What good would protesting do?

The only weapon she had to fight with was her talent behind the steering wheel.

Her father's time had been cruelly cut short, stamped out by vicious lies that had destroyed him and robbed her of the one person who had truly loved and believed in her.

Sasha was damned if she would let history repeat itself. Damned if she would give up her only chance to prove everyone wrong.

Gritting her teeth, she ignored his hand and stepped out of the car.

Marco strode across the marble foyer, the box clutched firmly in his grip. Its contents were a vivid reminder, stamped onto his brain.

Behind him he heard the hurried click of booted heels as Sasha Fleming struggled to keep up with him.

He didn't slow down. In fact he sped up. He wanted this meeting over with so he could return to the hospital.

For a single moment Marco thanked God his mother wasn't alive. She couldn't have borne to see her darling son, the miracle child she'd thought she'd never have, lying battered and bruised in a coma.

It was bad enough that she'd had to live through the pain and suffering Marco had brought her ten years ago. Bad enough that those horrendous three weeks before and after his own crash had caused a rift he'd never quite managed to heal, despite his mother's reassurances that all was well.

Marco knew all hadn't been well because *he* had never been the same since that time.

Deep shame and regret raked through him at how utterly he'd let his mother down. At how utterly he'd lost his grip on reality back then. Foolishly and selfishly he'd thought himself in love. The practised smile of a skilful manipulator had blinded him into throwing all caution to the wind and he'd damaged his family in the process.

His mother was gone, her death yet another heavy weight on his conscience, but Rafael was alive—and Marco intended to make sure lightning didn't strike twice. For that to happen he had to keep it together. He *would* keep it together.

'Um, the sign for the bar points the other way.'

Sasha Fleming's husky voice broke into his unwelcome thoughts.

He stopped so suddenly she bumped into him. Marco frowned at the momentary sensation of her breasts against his back and the unsuspecting heat that surged into his groin. His whole body tightened in furious rejection and he rounded on her.

'I don't conduct my business in bars. And I seriously doubt you want our conversation to be overheard by anyone else.'

Turning on his heel, he stalked to the lift. His personal porter pushed the button and waited for Marco to enter the express lift that serviced the presidential suite.

Sasha shot him a wary look and he bit back the urge to let a feral smile loose. Ever since Rafael's crash he'd been pushing back the blackness, fighting memories that had no place here within this chaos.

Really, Sasha Fleming had chosen the worst possible time to make herself his enemy. His hands tightened around the box and his gaze rested on her.

Run, he silently warned her. *While you have the chance.*

Her eyes searched every corner of the mirrored lift as if danger lurked within the gold-filigree-trimmed interior. Finally she rolled her shoulders. The subtle movement was almost the equivalent of cracking one's knuckles before a fight, and it intrigued him far more than he wanted to admit.

'We're going to your suite? Okay…'

She stepped into the lift. Behind her, Marco saw the porter's gaze drop to linger on her backside. Irritation rose to mingle with the already toxic cauldron of emotions swirling through him. With an impatient finger he stabbed at the button.

'I see the thought of it doesn't disturb you too much.' He didn't bother to conceal the slur in his comment. The urge to attack, to wound, ran rampage within him.

Silently he conceded she was right. As long as Rafael was fighting for his life he couldn't think straight. The impulse to make someone pay seethed just beneath the surface of his calm.

And Sasha Fleming had placed herself front and centre in his sights.

He expected her to flinch. To show that his words had hit a mark.

He wasn't prepared for her careless shrug. 'You're right. I don't really want our conversation to feed tomorrow's headlines. I'm pretty sure by now most of the media know you're staying here.'

'So you're not afraid to enter a strange man's suite?'

'Are you strange? I thought you were merely the engineering genius who designed the Espiritu DSII and the Cervantes Conquistador.'

'I'm immune to flattery, Miss Fleming, and any other form of coercion running through your pretty little head.'

'Shame. I was about to spout some seriously nerd-tastic info *guaranteed* to make you like me.'

'You'd be wasting your time. I have a team specially selected to deal with sycophants.'

His barb finally struck home. She inhaled sharply and lowered her gaze.

Marco caught himself examining the determined angle of her chin, the sensual line of her full lips. At the base of her neck her pulse fluttered under satin-smooth skin. Against his will, another wave of heat surged through him. He threw a mental bucket of cold water over it.

This woman belonged to his brother.

The lift opened directly onto the living room—a white and silver design that flowed outside onto the balcony overlooking the Danube. Marco bypassed the sweeping floor-to-ceiling windows, strode to the antique desk set against the velvet wall and put the box down.

Recalling its contents, he felt anger coalesce once more within him.

He turned to find Sasha Fleming at the window, a look of total awe on her face as she gazed at the stunning views of the Buda Hills and the Chain Bridge. He took a moment to study her.

Hers wasn't a classical beauty. In fact there was more of the rangy tomboy about her than a woman who was aware of her body. Yet her face held an arresting quality. Her lips were wide and undeniably sensual, and her limbs contained an innate grace when she moved that drew the eye. Her silky black hair, pulled into a loose ponytail at the back of her head, gleamed like a jet pool in the soft lighting. His gaze travelled over her neck, past shoulders that held a hint of delicacy and down to her chest.

The memory of her breasts against his back intruded. Against him she'd felt decidedly soft, although her body was lithe, holding a whipcord strength that didn't hide her subtle femininity. When he'd held her wrist in Rafael's hospital room her skin had felt supple, smooth like silk…

Sexual awareness hummed within him, unwelcome and unacceptable. Ruthlessly he cauterised it. Even if he'd been remotely interested in a woman such as this, flawed as she was, and without a moral bone in her body, *she* was the reason his brother had crashed.

Besides, poaching had never been his style.

'So, what would it take to convince you to keep me on?' She addressed him without taking her eyes from the view.

Annoyance fizzled through him.

'You're known for having relationships with your team mates.'

Her breath caught and she turned sharply from the window. Satisfaction oozed through him at having snagged her attention.

Satisfaction turned to surprise when once again she didn't evade the question. 'One team mate. A very long time ago.'

'He also crashed under extreme circumstances and lost his drive, I believe?'

A simple careful nod. 'He retired from motor racing, yes.'

'And his seat was then given to you?'

Her eyes narrowed. 'Your extrapolation is way off base if you think it has any bearing on what has happened with Rafael.'

'Isn't it curious that you bring chaos to every team you join? Are you an unlucky charm, Miss Fleming?'

'As a former racer yourself, I'm sure you're familiar with the facts—drivers crash on a regular basis. It's a reality of the sport. In fact, wasn't a crash what ended *your* racing career?'

For the second time in a very short while the reminder of events of ten years ago cut through him like the sharpest knife. Forcing the memories away, he folded his arms. 'It's *your* circumstances that interest me, not statistics. You dumped this other guy just before a race. This seems to be your *modus operandi*.'

Her chest lifted with her affronted breath. He struggled not to let his gaze drop. 'I resent that. I thought you ran your team on merit and integrity, not rumour and hypothesis.'

'Here's your chance to dispel the rumours. How many other team mates have you slept with?'

'I had a *relationship* with one. Derek and I went out for a while. Then it ended.'

'But this…relationship grew quite turbulent, I believe? So much so that it eventually destroyed his career while yours flourished?'

She snorted. 'I wouldn't say flourished, exactly. More like sweated and blooded.'

'But you did start out being a reserve driver on his team. And you did dump him when his seat became available to you?'

Marco watched her lips tighten, her chin angling in a way that drew his eyes to her smooth throat.

'It's obvious you've done your homework. But I didn't come here to discuss my personal life with you—which, as it happens, is really none of your business.'

'When it relates to *my* brother and *my* team it becomes my business. And your actions in the past three months have directly involved Rafael.' He reached for the box on the table. 'Do you know what's in this box?' he asked abruptly.

A wary frown touched her forehead. 'No. How would I?'

'Let me enlighten you. It contains the personal effects that were found on Rafael's person when he was pulled out of the car.' He opened the box. The inside was smeared with blood. Rafael's blood.

Blood he'd spilled because of this woman.

He lifted a gold chain with a tiny crucifix at the end of it. 'My mother gave this to him on the day of his confirmation, when he was thirteen years old. He always wears it during a race. For good luck.'

A look passed over her face. Sadness and a hint of guilt, perhaps? He dropped the chain back into the container, closed it and set it down. Reaching into his pocket, he produced another box—square, velvet.

She tensed, her eyes flaring with alarm. 'Mr de Cervantes—'

His lips twisted. 'You're not quite the talented actress I took you for, after all. Because your expression tells me everything I need to know. Rafael asked the question he'd been burning to ask, didn't he?' he demanded.

'I—'

He cut across her words, not at all surprised when the colour fled her face. 'My brother asked you to marry him. And you callously rejected him, knowing he would have to race directly afterwards. *Didn't you?*'

CHAPTER THREE

SASHA clenched her fists behind her back, desperately trying to hold it together. Even from across the room she could feel Marco's anger. It vibrated off his skin, slammed around the room like a living thing.

Her heart thudded madly in her chest. She opened her mouth but no words emerged.

'Here's your chance to speak up, Miss Fleming,' Marco incised, one long finger flipping open the box to reveal a large, stunning pink diamond set within a circle of smaller white diamonds.

She'd never been one to run from a fight, and Lord knew she'd had many fights in her life. But, watching Marco advance towards her, Sasha yearned to take a step back. Several steps, in fact…right out through the door. Unfortunately she chose that moment to look into his eyes.

The sheer force of his gaze trapped her. It held her immobile, darkly fascinating even as her panic flared higher. She'd dealt with disrespect, with disdain, even with open slurs against her.

Seething, pain-racked Spanish males like Marco de Cervantes were a different box of frogs.

'Did you refuse my brother or not?' he demanded, and his low, dangerous voice scoured her skin.

Suppressing a shiver, she said, 'You've got it wrong. Rafael didn't ask me—'

'Liar.' He snapped the box shut. 'He sent me a text last night. You said no.'

'Of course I said no. He didn't mean—'

He continued as if she hadn't spoken. 'He thought you were just playing hard to get. He was going to try again this morning.'

Sasha knew the brothers were close, but Rafael hadn't given her any indication he was *this* close to his brother. In fact the reason she'd grown close to him, despite his irreverent antics with the team and his wildly flirtatious behaviour with every female he came into contact with, was because she'd glimpsed the loneliness Rafael desperately tried to hide. Loneliness she'd identified with.

She watched Marco's nostrils flare with ever deepening anger as he waited for her answer. She licked her lips, carefully choosing her words, because it was clear that Rafael, for his own reasons, hadn't given Marco all the facts.

'Rafael and I are just friends.'

'Do you take me for a fool, Miss Fleming? You really expect me to believe that you viewed the romantic dinners for two in London or the spontaneous trip to Paris last month as innocent gestures of a mere friend?'

Another stab of surprise went through her at the depth of Marco's knowledge. 'I went to dinner with him because Rav... his date stood him up.'

'And Paris?'

'He was appearing at some function and I was at a loose end. I tagged along for laughs.'

'For laughs? And you then proceeded to dance the night away in his arms? What about the other half a dozen times you've been snapped together by the paparazzi?' he demanded.

She frowned. 'I know you two are close, but don't you think you're taking an alarmingly unhealthy interest in your brother's private life?'

His head jerked as if she'd slapped him. His hazel eyes darkened and his shoulders stiffened as if he held some dark emotion inside. Again she wanted to step back. To flee from a fight for the first time in her life.

'It's my duty to protect my brother,' he stated, with a finality that sharpened her interest.

'Rafael's a grown man. He doesn't need protecting.'

His raised a hand and slowly unfurled his fingers from around the velvet box. 'Then what do you call this? Why did my brother, the reigning world champion, who rarely ever makes mistakes, deliberately drive into the back of a slower car?'

Her gasp scoured her throat. 'The accident wasn't deliberate.' She refused to believe Rafael would have acted so recklessly. 'Rafael wouldn't put himself or another driver in such danger.'

'I've watched my brother race since he was six years old. His skill is legendary. He would never have put himself into the slipstream of a slower car so close to a blind corner. Not if he'd been thinking straight.'

Sasha couldn't refute the allegation because she'd wondered herself why Rafael had made such a dangerous move. 'Maybe he thought he could make the move stick,' she pursued half-heartedly.

Long bronze hands curled around the box. Features tight, Marco breathed deeply. 'Or maybe he didn't care. Maybe it was already too late for him when he stepped into the cockpit?'

Horror raked through her. 'Of course it wasn't. Why would you say that?'

'He sent me a text an hour before the race to tell me he intended to have what he wanted. *At all costs.*'

Sasha's blood ran cold. 'I…no, he couldn't have said that! Besides, he didn't mean—' She bit her lip to stop the rest of her words. Although they'd rowed, she wasn't about to betray Rafael's trust. 'We're just friends.'

'You're poison.' His hand slashed through the denial she'd been about to utter. 'Whatever thrall you hold over your fellow team mates, it ends right now.'

Sliding the box containing the engagement ring into his pocket, he returned to the desk. Several papers were spread across it. He searched through until he found what he was looking for.

'Your contract is a rolling one, due to end next season.'

Still reeling from the force of his words, Sasha stared at him.

'My lawyers will hammer out the finer details of a pay-off

in the next few days. But as of right now your services are no longer needed by Team Espiritu.'

With the force of a bucket of cold water, she was wrenched from her numbness.

'You're firing me because I befriended your brother?'

The hysterical edge to her voice registered on the outer fringes of her mind, but Sasha ignored it. She'd worked too hard, fought too long for this chance to let mere hysteria stand in her way. If she had to scream like a banshee she would do so to make Marco de Cervantes listen to her. After years of withstanding vicious whispers and callous undermining, she would not be dismissed so easily. Not when her chance to see her father's reputation restored, the chance to prove her own worth, was so close.

'Do you want to stop for a moment and think how absurd that is? Do you really want to carry on down that road?' she demanded, raising her chin when he turned from the desk.

'What road?' he asked without looking up.

'The sexist, discriminatory road. Or are you going to fire Rafael too when he wakes up? Just to even things up?'

His gaze hardened. 'I've been running this team for almost a decade and no one has ever been allowed to cause this much disruption unchecked before.'

'What do you mean, unchecked?'

'I warned Rafael about you three months ago,' he delivered without an ounce of remorse. 'I told him you were trouble. That he should stay away from you.'

Her anger blazed into an inferno. 'How dare you?'

He merely shrugged. 'Unfortunately, with Rafael, you only have to suggest there's something he can't have to make him hunger desperately for it.'

'You're unbelievable—you know that? You think you can play with people's lives!'

His face darkened. 'Believe me, I'm not playing. Five million.'

Confused, she frowned. 'Five million...for what?'

'To walk away. Dollars, pounds or euros. It doesn't really matter.'

Fire crackled inside her. 'You want to pay me to give up my seat? To disappear like some sleazy secret simply because I became friends with your brother? Even to a wild nut-job like me that seems very drastic. What exactly are you afraid of, Mr de Cervantes?'

Strong, corded arms folded over his chest. His body was held so tense she feared he would snap a muscle at any second. 'Let's just say I have experience with women like you.'

'Damn, I thought I was one of a kind. Would you care to elaborate on that stunning assertion?'

One brow winged upward. 'And have you selling the story to the first tabloid hack you find? I'll pass. Five million. To resign and to stay away from the sport.'

'Go to hell.' She added a smile just for the hell of it, because she yearned for him to feel a fraction of the anger and humiliation coursing through her. The same emotions her father had felt when he'd been thrown out of the profession that had been his life.

'Is that your final answer?' he asked.

'Yes. I don't need to phone a friend and I don't need to ask any audience. My final answer—*go to hell!*'

Sasha braced herself for more of the backlash he'd been doling out solidly for the last hour. But all he did was stare at her, his gaze once again leaving her feeling exposed, as if he'd stripped back a layer of her skin.

He nodded once. Then he paced the room, seemingly lost for words. Finally he raked both hands through his hair, ruffling it until the silky strands looked unkempt in a sexy, just-got-out-of-bed look that she couldn't help but stare at.

Puzzled by his attitude, she forced her gaze away and tried to hang on to her anger. She didn't deserve this. All she'd tried to be was a friend to Rafael, a team mate who'd seemed to be battling demons of his own.

After her experience with Derek, and the devastating pain of losing the baby she hadn't known she was carrying until it was too late, she'd vowed never to mix business with pleasure. Derek's jealousy as she'd risen through the ranks of the racing world had eroded any feelings she'd had for him until there'd been nothing left.

As if sensing her withdrawal, he'd tried to hang on to her with a last-ditch proposal. When she'd turned him down he'd labelled her a bitch and started a whispering campaign against her that had undermined all her years of hard work.

Thankfully Derek had never found out the one thing he could have used against her. The one thing that could have shattered her very existence. The secret memory of her lost baby was buried deep inside, where no one could touch it or use it as a weapon against her.

Even her father hadn't known, and after living through his pain and humiliation she'd vowed never to let her personal life interfere with her work ever again.

Rafael's easy smile and wildly charming ways had got under her guard, making her reveal a few careful details about her past to him. His friendship had been a balm to the lonely existence she'd lived as Jack Fleming's daughter.

The thought that Marco had poisoned him against her filled her with sadness.

'You know, I thought it was Rafael who told *you* about my past. But it was the other way round, wasn't it?' she asked.

She waited for his answer, but his gaze was fixed on the view outside, on the picturesque towers of the Royal Castle. A stillness surrounded him that caught and held her attention.

'For as long as I can remember I've been bailing Rafael out of one scrape or another.'

The words—low, intense and unexpected—jolted aside her anger.

'He's insanely passionate about every single aspect of his life, be it food, driving or volcano-boarding down the side of some godforsaken peak in Nicaragua,' he continued. 'Unfortunately the perils of this world seem to dog him. When he was eleven, he discovered mushrooms growing in a field at our vineyard in León and decided to eat them. His stomach had to be pumped or he'd have died. Two years later, he slipped away from his boarding school to run with the bulls at Pamplona. He was gored in the arm. Save for a very substantial donation to the school, and my personal guarantee of his reformation, he would've been thrown out immediately.'

His gaze focused on her. 'I can list another dozen episodes that would raise your hair.'

'He's a risk-taker,' Sasha murmured, wondering where the conversation was headed but deciding to go with it. 'He has to be as a racing driver; surely you understand that?' she argued. 'Didn't you scale Everest on your own five years ago, after everyone in your team turned back because of a blizzard? In my book that's Class A recklessness.'

'I knew what I was doing.'

'Oh, okay. How about continuing over half the London-Dakar rally with a broken arm?'

His clear surprise made her lips twist. 'How—?'

'Told you I had nerd-tastic info on you. You own the most successful motor racing team in the history of the sport. I want to drive for you. I've done my homework.'

'Very impressive, but risk-taking on the track is expected—within reason. But even before Rafael ever got behind the wheel of a race car he was…highly strung.'

'If he's so highly strung that you have to manage him, then why do you let him race? Why own the team that places him in the very sport likely to jeopardise his well-being?'

His eyes darkened and he seemed to shut off. Watching him, Sasha was fascinated by the impenetrable mask that descended over his face.

'Because racing is in our blood. It's what we do. My father never got the chance to become a racer. I raced for him, but because I had the talent. So does Rafael. There was never any question that racing was our future. But it's also my job to take care of my brother. To save him from himself. To make him see beyond his immediate desires.'

'Have you thought that perhaps if you let him make his own mistakes instead of trying to manage his life he'll wise up eventually?'

'So far, no.'

'He's a grown man. When are you going to cut the apron strings?'

'When he's proved to me that he won't kill himself without them.'

'And are you so certain you can save him every single time?'

'I can put safety measures in place.'

She laughed at his sheer arrogance. 'You're not omnipotent. You can't control what happens in life. Even if you could, Rafael will eventually resent you for controlling his life.'

Marco's lips firmed, his eyelids descending to veil his eyes.

She gave another laugh. 'He already does, doesn't he? Did you two fight? Was that why you weren't at the track this weekend?'

He ignored her questions. 'What I do, I do for his own good. And you're not good for him. My offer still stands.'

Just like that they were back to his sleazy offer of a buy-off. Distaste filled her.

She looked around the sleekly opulent room at the highly polished surfaces, the velvet walls, the bespoke furniture and elegant, sweeping staircases that belonged more in a stately home than in a hotel. Luxurious decadence only people like Marco de Cervantes could afford. The stamp of power and authority told her she wouldn't find even the smallest chink in the de Cervantes armour.

The man was as impenetrable as his wealth was immeasurable.

In the end, all she could rely on was her firm belief in right and wrong.

'You can't fire me simply to keep me out of Rafael's way. It's unethical. I think somewhere deep down you know it too.'

'I don't need moral guidance from someone like you.'

'I disagree. I think you need a big-ass, humongous compass. Because you're making a big mistake if you think I'm going to go quietly.'

His smile didn't quite reach his eyes. 'Rafael told me you were feisty.'

What else had Rafael told him? Decidedly uncomfortable at the thought of being the subject of discussion, she shrugged.

'I haven't reached where I am today without a fight or three. I won't go quietly,' she stressed again.

Several minutes of silence stretched. Her nerves stretched along with them. Just when she thought she'd break, that she'd have to resort to plain, old-fashioned, humiliating begging, he hitched one taut-muscled thigh over the side of the desk and indicated the chair in front of it.

'Sit down. I think a discussion is in order.'

Marco watched relief wash over her face and hid a triumphant smile.

He'd never had any intention of firing Sasha Fleming. Not immediately, anyway. He'd wanted her rattled, on a knife-edge at the possibility of losing what was evidently so precious to her.

The bloodthirsty, vengeance-seeking beast inside him felt a little appeased at seeing her shaken. He also wanted to test her, to see how far she would go to fight for what she wanted. After all, the higher the value she placed on her career, the sweeter it would be to snatch it away from her. Just as he'd had everything wrenched from *him* ten years ago.

He ruthlessly brushed aside the reminder of Angelique's betrayal and focused on Sasha as she walked towards him.

Again his senses reacted to her in ways that made his jaw clench. The attraction—and, yes, he was man enough to admit to it—was unwelcome as much as it was abhorrent. Rafael was in a coma, fighting for his life. The last thing Marco wanted to acknowledge was a chemical reaction to the woman in the middle of all this chaos. To acknowledge how the flare of her hips made his palms itch to shape them. How the soft lushness of her lower lip made him want to caress his finger over it.

'Regardless of the state of the team, I have a responsibility towards the sponsors.'

His office had already received several calls, ostensibly expressing concern for his brother's welfare. In truth the sponsors were sniffing around, desperate to find out what Marco's next move would be—specifically, who he would put in Rafael's place and how it would affect their bottom line.

She nodded. 'Rafael was scheduled to appear at several sponsored engagements during the August hiatus. They'll want to know what's happening.'

Once again Marco was struck by the calm calculation in her voice. This wasn't the tone of a concerned lover or a distraught team mate. Her mind was firmly focused on Team Espiritu. In other circumstances, her single-mindedness would have been admirable. But he knew first-hand the devastation ambition like hers could wreak.

Before he could answer a knock sounded on his door. One of his two butlers materialised from wherever he'd been stationed and opened the door.

Russell Latchford, his second-in-command, and Luke Green, the team's chief engineer, entered.

Russell approached. 'I've just been to see Rafael—' He stopped when he saw Sasha. 'Sasha. I didn't know you were here.' His tone echoed the question in his eyes.

Sasha returned his gaze calmly. Nothing ruffled her. Nothing except the threatened loss of her job. The urge to see her lose that cool once again attacked Marco's senses.

'Miss Fleming's here to discuss future possibilities in light of Rafael's accident.'

As team principal, it was Russell's job to source the best drivers for the team, with Marco giving final approval. Marco saw his disgruntlement, but to his credit Russell said nothing.

'Have you brought the shortlist I asked for?' Marco asked Russell.

Sasha inhaled sharply, and he saw her hands clench in her lap as Russell handed over a piece of paper.

'I've already been discreetly approached by the top five, but every driver in the sport wants to drive for us. It'll cost you to buy out their contracts, of course. If you go for someone from the lower ranking teams it'll still cost you, but the fallout won't be as damaging as poaching someone from the top teams.'

Marco shook his head. 'Our sponsors signed up for the package—Rafael and the car. I don't want a second-class driver.

I need someone equally talented and charismatic or the sponsors will throw hissy fits.'

Luke spoke up. 'There's also the problem of limited in-season testing. We can't just throw in a brand-new driver mid-season and expect him to handle the car anywhere near the way Rafael did.'

Marco glanced down at the list. 'No. Rafael is irreplaceable. I accept that the Drivers' Championship is no longer an option, but I want to win the Constructors' Championship. The team deserves it. All of these drivers would ditch their contract to drive for me, but I'd rather not deal with a messy court battle. Where do we stand on the former champion who retired last year? Have you contacted him?'

Russell shook his head. 'Even with the August break he won't be in good enough shape when the season resumes in September.'

'So my only option is to take on a driver from another team?'

'No, it isn't.' Sasha's voice was low, but intensely powerful, and husky enough to command attention.

Marco's eyes slid to her. Her stance remained relaxed, one leg crossed over the other, but in her eyes he saw ferocious purpose.

'You have something to add?'

Fierce blue eyes snapped at him as she rolled her shoulders. As last time, he couldn't help but follow the movement. Then his eyes travelled lower, to the breasts covered by her nondescript T-shirt. Again the pull of desire was strong and sharp, unlike anything he'd experienced before. Again he pushed it away and forced his gaze back to her face.

A faint flush covered her cheeks. 'You know I do. I know the car inside out. I've driven it at every Friday Practice since last season. The way I see it, I'm the only way you can win the Constructors' Championship. Plus you'd save a lot of money and the unnecessary litigation of trying to tempt away a driver mid-season from another team. In the last few practices my run-times have nearly equalled Rafael's.'

Marco silently admitted the truth of her words. He might not sit on the pit wall for every single minute of a race—the engineer and aerodynamicist in him preferred the hard facts of the telemetry reports—but he knew Sasha's race times to the last fraction.

He also knew racing was more than just the right car in the right hands. 'Yes, but you're yet to perform under the pressure of a Saturday practice, a pole position shoot-out and a race on Sunday. I'd rather have a driver with actual race experience.'

Russell fidgeted and cleared his throat. 'I agree, Marco. I think Alan might be a better option—'

'I've consistently surpassed Alan's track times,' she said of the team's second driver. 'Luke will confirm it.'

Luke's half-hearted shrug made Marco frown.

'Is there a problem?'

The other man cleared his throat. 'Not a problem, exactly, but I'm not sure how the team will react to…you know…'

'No, I don't know. If you have something to say, then say it.'

'He means how the team will react to a woman lead driver,' Sasha stated baldly.

Recalling her accusation of sexism, he felt a flash of anger swell through him. He knew the views of others when it came to employing women as drivers. The pathetically few women racers attested to the fact that it was a predominantly male sport, but he believed talent was talent, regardless of the gender that wielded it.

The thought that key members in his team didn't share his belief riled him.

He rose. 'That will be all, gentlemen.'

Russell's surprise was clear. 'Do you need some time to make the decision?'

His gaze stayed on Sasha. Her chest had risen in a sharp intake of breath. Again he had to force himself not to glance down at her breasts. The effort it took not to look displeased him immensely.

'I've requested figures from my lawyers by morning. I'll let you know my decision.'

His butler led them out.

'Mr de Cervantes—' Sasha started.

He held up a hand. 'Let me make one thing clear. I didn't

refuse you a drive because of your gender. Merely because of your disruptive influence within my team.'

Her eyes widened, then she nodded. 'Okay. But I want to—'

'I need to return to my brother's bedside. You'll also find out my decision tomorrow.' He turned to leave.

'Please. I…need this.'

The raw, fervent emotion in her voice stopped him from leaving the room. Returning to her side, he stared down at her bent head. Her hands were clenched tighter. A swathe of pure black hair had slipped its knot and half covered her face. His fingers itched to catch it back, smooth it behind her ear so he could see her expression.

Most of all, he wanted her to look at him.

'Why? Why is this so important to you?' he asked.

'I…I made a promise.' Her voice was barely above a whisper.

Marco frowned. 'A promise? To whom?'

She inhaled, and before his eyes she gathered herself in. Her spine straightened, and her shoulders snapped back until her whole body became poised, almost regal. Then her eyes slowly rose to his.

The steely determination in their depths compelled his attention. His blood heated, rushing through his veins in a way that made his body clench in denial. Yet he couldn't look away.

Her gaze dropped. Marco bit back the urge to order her to look at him.

'It doesn't matter. All you need to know is if you give me a chance I'll hand you the Constructors' Championship.'

Sasha heard the low buzzing and cursed into her pillow. How the blazes had a wasp got into her room?

And since when did wasps make such a racket?

Groaning, she rolled over and tried to burrow into a better position. Sleep had been an elusive beast. She'd spent the night alternately pacing the floor and running through various arguments in her head about how she would convince Marco to keep her on the team. In the end exhaustion had won out.

Now she'd been woken by—

Her phone! With a yelp, she shoved off the covers and stumbled blindly for the satchel she'd discarded on the floor.

'Huhn?'

'Do I take it by that unladylike grunt that I've disturbed your sleep?' Marco de Cervantes's voice rumbled down the line.

'Not at all,' she lied. 'What time is it?' She furiously rubbed her eyes. She'd never been a morning person.

Taut silence, then, 'It's nine-thirty.'

'What? *Damn.*' She'd slept through her alarm. Again.

Could anyone blame her, though? Being part of Team Espiritu meant staying in excellent accommodation, but this time management had excelled itself—the two thousand thread-count cotton sheets, handmade robes, the hot tub, lotions and potions, the finest technology and her personal maid on tap were just the beginnings of the absurd luxury that made the crew of Marco's team the envy of the circuit. But her four-poster bed and its mattress—dear Lord, the made-by-angels mattress—was the reason—

'Do you have somewhere else to be, Miss Fleming?'

'Yes. I have a plane to catch back to London at eleven.' Thankfully she didn't have a lot of things to pack, having put her restless energy to good use last night. And the airport was only ten minutes away. Still, she was cutting it fine.

'You might wish to revise that plan.'

She froze, refusing to acknowledge the thin vein of hope taking root deep within her. 'And why would I need to do that?'

'I have a proposition for you. Open your door.'

'What?'

'Open your door. I need to look into your eyes when I outline my plan so there can be no doubt on either part.'

'You're *here*?' Her eyes darted to her door, as if she could see his impressive body outlined through the solid wood.

'I'm here. But I'll soon be a figment of your imagination if you don't open your door.'

Sasha glanced down at herself. No way was she opening the door to Marco de Cervantes wearing a vampire T-shirt that de-

clared *'Bite Me'* in blood-red. And she didn't even want to think
of the state of her hair.

'I… Can you give me two minutes?' If she could get in and
out of a race suit in ninety seconds, she sure as hell could make
herself presentable in a fraction of that time.

'You have five seconds. Then I move on to my next call.'

'No. Wait!' Keeping the phone glued to her ear, she rushed
to the door. Pulling it open, she stuck her head out, trying her
best to shield the rest of her body from full view.

And there he stood. Unlike the casual clothes of yesterday,
Marco was dressed in a bespoke suit, his impressive shoulders
even more imposing underneath the slate-grey jacket, blue shirt
and pinstriped tie, his long legs planted in battle stance. His hair
was combed neatly, unlike the unruly, sexy mess it'd been yesterday. The strong desire to see it messy again had her pulling
back a fraction.

Eyes locked on hers, he lowered his phone. 'Invite me in.'

'Why? Are you a vampire?' she shot back, then swallowed
a groan.

Frown lines creased his brow. *'Excuse me?* Are you high?'

Sasha silently cursed her morning brain. 'Hah—I wish. Oh,
never mind. I'm…I'm not really dressed to receive guests, but I
didn't want you to leave, so unless you want to extend that five-
second ultimatum this will have to do.'

His frown deepened. 'Are you in the habit of answering your
hotel door naked?'

Heat crawled up her neck and stung her face. 'Of course not.
I'm not naked.'

'Prove it' came the soft challenge.

'Fine. See?' Belatedly she wondered at her sanity as she
stepped into his view and felt the dark, intense force of Marco's
gaze as it travelled over her.

When his eyes returned to hers, the breath snagged in her
lungs. His hazel eyes had darkened to burnt gold with dark
green flecks; the clench of his jaw was even more pronounced.
He seemed to be straining against an emotion that was more
than a little bit frightening.

She stepped back. He followed her in and shut the door. The luxury hotel suite that had seemed so vast, so over the top, closed in on her. She took another step back. He followed, eyes locked on her.

Her phone fell from her fingers, thankfully cushioned by the shag-pile carpet. Mouth dry, she kept backing up. He kept following.

'I make it a point not to credit rumours, but it seems in this instance the rumours are true, Sasha Fleming.'

The way he said her name—slowly, with a hint of Latin intonation—made goosebumps rise on her flesh. Her nipples peaked and a sensation she recognised to her horror as desire raked through her abdomen, sending delicious darts of liquid heat to the apex of her thighs.

'What exactly do you think is true about me?'

'Sex is your weapon of choice,' he breathed, his eyes lingering on the telltale nubs beneath her T-shirt. 'The only trouble is you wield it so unsubtly.'

'I beg your pardon?' she squeaked as the backs of her legs touched the side of the bed. 'Did you just say—?'

'You need to learn to finesse your art.'

'What in heaven's name are you blathering about? Are you sure *you're* not the one who's high?' she flung back.

'No man likes to be bludgeoned over the head with sex. No matter how...enticing the package.'

'You're either loopy or you've got me confused with someone else. I don't bludgeon and I don't entice.'

He kept coming.

She leaned back on the bed and felt the hem of her shirt riding up her thighs. 'For goodness' sake, stop!'

He stopped, but his gaze didn't. It continued its destructive course over her, leaving no part of her untouched, until Sasha felt sure she was about to combust from the heat of it.

Desperate, she let her tongue dart out to lick her lips. 'Look... Derek—I presume that's where you got your little morsel from— said a lot of unsavoury things about me when we broke up. But I'm not who...whatever you think I am.'

'Even though I can see the evidence for myself?' he rasped in a low voice.

She scrambled over the side of the bed and grabbed the robe she'd dropped on the floor last night. With shaking fingers, and a mind scrambling to keep pace with the bizarre turn of the conversation, she pulled the lapels over her traitorous body.

Having pursued her profession in fast cars financed by billionaires with unlimited funds, Sasha knew there was a brand of women who found the whole X1 Premier Racing world a huge turn-on: women who used their sexuality to pursue racers with a single-mindedness that bordered on the obsessive.

She'd never considered for a second that she would ever be bracketed with them—especially by the wealthiest, most sought-after billionaire of them all. The idea would have been laughable if the sting of Derek's betrayal still didn't have the ability to hurt.

'Well, whatever it is you *think* you see, there's no truth to the rumour. Now, can we please get back to the reason you came here in the first place?'

Her words seemed to rouse him from whatever dark, edgy place he'd been in. He looked up from her thighs, slowly exhaled, and looked around the room, taking in the rumpled bed and the contents of her satchel strewn on the floor.

When he paced to the window and drew back the curtain she took the opportunity to tie the robe tighter around her, hoping it would dispel the electricity zinging around her body.

He turned after a minute, his face devoid of expression. 'I've decided not to recruit a new driver. Doing so mid-season is not financially viable. Besides, they all have contracts and sponsorship commitments to fulfil.'

Hope grew so powerful it weakened her legs. Sinking down onto the side of the bed, she swallowed. 'So, does that mean I have the seat for the rest of the season?'

He shoved his hands into his pockets, his gaze fixed squarely on her. 'You'll sign an agreement promising to honour every commitment the team holds you to. Half of the sponsors have agreed to let you fulfil Rafael's commitments.'

He hadn't given a definite *yes*, but Sasha's heartbeat thundered nonetheless. 'And the other half?'

'With nowhere to go, they'll come round. My people are working on them.'

Unable to stem the flood of emotion rising inside, she pried her gaze from his and stared down at her trembling hands. She struggled to breathe.

Finally. The chance to wipe the slate clean. To earn the respect that had been ruthlessly denied her and so callously wrenched from her father. Finally the Fleming name would be spoken of with esteem and not disdain. Jack Fleming would be allowed to rest in peace, his legacy nothing to be ashamed of any more.

'I...thank you,' she murmured.

'You haven't heard the conditions attached to your drive.'

She shook her head, careless of the hair flying about her face as euphoria frothed inside her. 'I agree. Whatever it is, I agree.' She wouldn't let this opportunity slip her by. She intended to grab it with both hands. To prove to anyone who'd dared to naysay that they'd been wrong.

His eyes narrowed. 'Yesterday you promised to give *anything* not to have Rafael in hospital. Today you're agreeing to conditions you haven't even heard. Are you always this carefree with your consent? Perhaps I need to rethink making you lead driver. I shudder to think what such rashness could cost me on the race track.'

'I... Fine—name your conditions.'

He quirked a mocking brow. '*Gracias.* Aside from the other commitments, there are two that I'm particularly interested in. Team Espiritu *must* win the Constructors' Championship. We're eighty points ahead of the next championship challenger. I expect those points only to go up. Understood?'

A smile lit up her face. 'Absolutely. I intend to wipe the floor with them.'

'The second condition—'

'Wait. I have a condition of my own.'

His lips twisted. '*Déjà vu* overwhelms me. I suppose I shouldn't be surprised.'

Sasha ignored him, the need to voice a wish so long denied making her words trip from her lips with a life of their own. 'If...*when* I secure you the Constructors' Championship, I want my contract with Team Espiritu to be extended for another year.'

When his eyes narrowed further, she rushed to speak again.

'You can write it into my contract that I'll be judged based on my performance during the next three months. If we win the Constructors' you'll hire me for another year.'

'Winning a Drivers' Championship means that much to you?'

His curiously flat tone drew her gaze, but his expression remained inscrutable. Her heart hammered with the force of her deepest yearning. 'Yes, it does.'

His eyelids descended, veiling his gaze. The tension in the room increased until she could cut the atmosphere with a butter knife. But when he looked back up there was nothing but cool, impersonal regard.

'Very well. Win the Constructors' Championship and I'll extend your contract for another year.'

She couldn't believe he'd agreed so readily. 'Wow, that was easy.'

'Perhaps it's because I don't believe in talking every subject to death. My time is precious.'

'Yes, of course...'

'As I was saying, before you interrupted, my second condition is more important, Miss Fleming, so listen carefully. You'll have no personal contact with any male member of the team; you will go nowhere near my brother. Any hint of a non-professional relationship with another driver or anyone within the sport, for that matter, will mean instant dismissal. And I'll personally make it my mission to ensure you never drive another racing car. Do we understand each other?'

CHAPTER FOUR

'IF YOU'VE finished your breakfast, I'll take you on the tour of the race track.'

Sasha looked up from her almost empty plate of scrambled eggs and ham to find Marco lounging in the doorway that connected the vast living room to the sun-drenched terrace of *Casa de Leon*.

She'd been here three days, and she still couldn't get her head round the sheer vastness of the de Cervantes estate. Navigating her way around the huge, rambling two-storey villa without getting lost had taken two full days.

With its white stucco walls, dark red slate roofs and large cathedral-like windows, *Casa de Leon* was an architect's dream. The high exposed beams, sweeping staircases and intricately designed marble floors wouldn't have been out of place in a palace. Every piece of furniture, painting and drape looked as if it cost a fortune. Even the air inside the villa smelled different, tinged with a special rarefied, luxurious quality that made her breath catch.

Outside, an endless green vista, broken only by perfectly manicured gardens, stretched as far as the eye could see... It was no wonder the countless villa staff travelled around in golf buggies.

Realising Marco was waiting for an answer, she nodded, drawing her gaze from the long, muscular legs encased in dark grey trousers. 'Sure. I'll just finish my coffee. Aren't you hav-

ing anything?' She indicated the mouth-watering spread of sea-
sonal fruit, pastries and ham slices on the table.

Disengaging himself from the doorway, he came towards her,
powerfully sleek and oozing arrogant masculinity. 'I'll have a
coffee, too.'

When he sat and made no move to pour it himself, she raised
an eyebrow. 'Yes, boss. Three bags full, boss?'

His hazel eyes gleamed and Sasha had the distinct feeling
he was amused, although not a smile cracked his lips. In fact he
looked decidedly strained. Which wasn't surprising under the
circumstances, she reminded herself.

Feeling the mutiny give way, she poured him a cup. 'Black?'

'*Sí*. Two sugars.'

She looked up, surprised. 'Funny, I wouldn't have pegged
you for the two-sugars type.'

'And how *would* you have pegged me?'

'Black, straight up, drunk boiling hot without a wince.'

'Because my insides are made of tar and my soul is black as
night?' he mocked.

She shrugged. 'Hey, you said it.' She added sugar and passed
it over.

'*Gracias.*' He picked up a silver spoon and stirred his drink,
the tiny utensil looking very delicate in his hand.

Sasha found herself following the movement, her gaze tracing the short dark hairs on the back of his hand. Suddenly her
mouth dried, and her stomach performed that stupid flip again.
Wrenching her gaze from the hypnotic motion, she picked up
her cup with a decidedly unsteady hand.

'How are you settling in?' he asked.

'Do you really want to know?'

The speed with which Marco had whisked her from Budapest
to Spain after she'd signed the contract had made her head spin.
Of course his luxury private jet—which he'd piloted himself—
had negated the tedium of long airport waits and might have
had something to do with it. They'd flown to Barcelona, then
transferred by helicopter to his estate in Leon.

He took another sip. 'I wouldn't have asked otherwise. You should know by now that I never say anything I don't mean.'

Now she felt surly. Her suite was the last word in luxury, complete with four-poster bed, half a dozen fluffy pillows and a deep-sunken marble bath to die for. Just across from where she sat, past the giant-sized terracotta potted plants and a barbecue area, an Olympic-sized swimming pool sparkled azure in the dappling morning light. She'd already sampled its soothing comfort, along with the sports gym equipped with everything she needed to keep her exercise regime on track. In reality, she wanted for nothing.

And yet…

'It's fine. I have everything I need. Thank you,' she tagged on waspishly. Then, wisely moving on before she ventured into full-blown snark, she asked, 'How is Rafael?'

Marco's gaze cooled.

Sasha sighed. 'I agreed to stay away from him. I didn't agree to stop caring about him.'

'The move from Budapest went fine. He's now in the care of the best Spanish doctors in Barcelona.'

'Since you'll probably bite my head off if I ask you to send him my best, I'll move on. How far away is the race track?'

'Three miles south.' Lifting his cup, he drained it.

'Exactly how big is this place?'

When Marco had announced he was bringing a skeleton team to Spain to help her train for her debut at the end of August, she'd mistakenly thought she would be spending most of her time in a race simulator. The half an hour it'd taken to travel from Marco's landing strip to his villa had given her an inkling of how immense his estate was.

His gaze pinned on her, he picked up an orange and skilfully peeled it. 'All around? About twenty-five square miles.'

'And you and Rafael own all of it?'

'*Sí.*' He popped a segment into his mouth.

Sasha carefully set her cup down, her senses tingling with warning. That soft *sí* had held a slight edge to it that made her wary. His next words confirmed her wariness.

'Just think, if only you'd said yes all this would've been yours.'

She didn't need to ask what he meant. Affecting a light tone, she toyed with the delicate handle of her expensive bone china cup. 'Gee, I don't know. The race track would've been handy, but what the hell would I do with the rest of the... What else is there, anyway?'

His gaze was deceptively lazy—deceptive because she could feel the charged animosity rising from him.

'There's a fully functioning vineyard and winery. And the stables house some of the best Andalucian thoroughbreds in Spain. There's also an exclusive by-invitation-only resort and spa on the other side of the estate.'

'Well, there you have it, then. My palate is atrociously common—not to mention that if I drink more than one glass of wine I get a raging headache. As for thoroughbreds—I couldn't tell you which end of the horse to climb if you put me next to one. So, really, you're way better off without me in your family. The spa sounds nice, though. A girl could always do with a foot rub after a hard day's work—although I have a feeling the amount of grease I tend to get under my nails would frighten your resort staff.'

A tiny tic appeared at his temple. 'Are you always this facetious, or do you practice?'

'Normally I keep it well hidden. I only show off when asked really, really nicely,' she flung back. Then she stood. 'From the unfortunate downturn of this conversation, I take it the offer of a tour is now off the table?' She tilted her chin, determined not to reveal how deep his barbs had stung.

'As much as I'm tempted to reward your petulance with time on the naughty step, that will only prove counterproductive.' Wiping his hands on a napkin, he rose to tower over her. 'You're here to train. Familiarising yourself with the race track is part of that training. I'll leave the naughty step for another time.'

Wisely deciding to leave the mention of the naughty step alone, Sasha relaxed her grip on the back of the chair. 'Thank you.'

Sasha followed him into the villa, staunchly maintaining her silence. But not talking didn't equate to not looking, and, damn it, she couldn't help but be intensely aware of the man beside her. His smell assailed her nostrils—that sharp tang of citrus coupled with the subtle undertones of musk that shifted as it flowed over his warmth.

Against the strong musculature of his torso his white polo shirt lovingly followed the superb lines of a deep chest and powerful shoulders. All that magnificence tapered down to a trim waist that knew not an ounce of fat.

Judging by his top-notch physicality, she wasn't surprised Marco had been the perfect championship-winning driver ten years ago.

'Why did you give up racing? You resigned so abruptly, and yet it's obvious you recovered fully after your crash.'

She saw his shoulders tense before he rounded on her. The icy, forbidding look in his eyes made her bite her lip.

Nice one, Sasha.

'That is not a subject up for discussion, Miss Fleming. And before you take it into your head to go prying I caution you against it. Understood?'

He barely waited for her nod before he wrenched open the front door.

Outside, two golf buggies sat side by side at the bottom of the steps. She headed towards the nearest one.

'Where are you going?' he bit out.

She stopped. 'Oh, I thought we were going by road.'

He nodded to the helipad, where a black and red chopper sat gleaming in the morning sun. 'We're touring by helicopter.'

It was a spectacularly beautiful machine—the latest in a long line of beautiful aircraft.

'Any chance you'll let me fly it?'

He flashed a mirthless grin at her. 'I don't see any pigs flying, do you?'

'Wow, this is incredible! How long have you had this race track?'

Marco glanced up from the helicopter controls, then immediately wished he hadn't. It was bad enough hearing her excitement piped directly into his headphones. The visual effects were even more disturbing.

When he'd offered her an aerial tour of the race track he hadn't taken into account how she was dressed. In most respects, her white shorts could be described as sensible—almost boyish. He'd been out with women who wore far less on a regular basis. Her light green shirt was also plain to the point of being utilitarian.

All the same, Marco found the combination of her excitement and her proximity...*aggravating*. Even more aggravating were the flashbacks he kept having of her leaning back on the bed in her hotel room, her T-shirt riding up to reveal skin so tempting it had knocked his breath clean out of his lungs...

Her naked ambition and her sheer drive to succeed were living things that charged the air around her. Marco knew only too well the high cost of blind ambition, and yet knowing the depths of Sasha Fleming's ambition and what she would do to achieve her goals didn't stop him from imagining how it would have felt to lift her T-shirt higher...just a fraction...

He was also more than a little puzzled that she'd made no attempt to gain his attention since that episode in her room. Women flaunted themselves at him at every opportunity— used every excuse in the book to garner his interest. Some even resorted to...*unconventional* means. Most of the time he was happy to direct them Rafael's way. He'd long outgrown the paddock bunny phase; had outgrown it even before Angelique, the most calculating of them all, had stepped into his orbit and turned his world upside down.

Marco sobered, seething at himself for the memories he suddenly couldn't seem to dispel so easily. Focusing on the controls, he banked the chopper and followed the straights and curves of the race track hundreds of metres below.

'I built it ten years ago,' he clipped out in answer to her question.

'After you retired?' she asked, surprised.

'No. Just before.' His harsh response had the desired effect of shutting her up, but when he glanced at her again, he noted the spark of speculation in her eyes. Before he could think about why he was doing so, he found himself elaborating. 'I thought I'd be spending more time here.' He'd woven foolish dreams about what his life would be like, how perfect everything had seemed. He'd had the perfect car; the perfect woman.

'What happened?'

The crushing pain of remembrance tightened around his chest. 'I crashed.'

She gave a sad little understanding nod that made him want to growl at her. What did she know? She was as conniving as they came.

Forcing his anger under control, he flew over the track towards the mid-point hill.

Sasha pointed to six golf buggies carrying mechanics who hopped out at various points of the track. 'What are they doing?'

'The track hasn't been used for a while. They're conducting last-minute checks on the moveable parts to make sure they're secure.'

'I can't believe this track can be reshaped to simulate other tracks around the circuit. I can't wait to have a go!'

Excitement tinged her voice and Marco couldn't help glancing over at her. Her eyes were alight with a smile that seemed to glow from within. His hands tightened around the controls.

'The track was built before simulators became truly effective. One concrete track would've served only to make a driver expert at a particular track, so I designed an interchangeable track. The other advantage is experience gained in driving on tarmac, or as close to tarmac—as you can get. Wet or dry conditions can make or break a race. This way the driver gets to practise on both with the right tyres. Electronic simulators and wind tunnels have their places, but so does this track.'

The helicopter crested another small hill and cold sweat broke out over his skin. Several feet to the side of the track a mound of whitewashed stones had been piled high in a makeshift monument. Marco's hand tightened on the lever and deftly swerved the aircraft away from the landmark he had no wish to see up close.

'Trust me, I'm not complaining. It's a great idea. I'm just surprised other teams haven't copied the idea. Or sold their first-
born sons to use your track.'

'Offers have been made in the past.'

'And?'

He shrugged. 'I occasionally allow them to use the track I
designed. But for the whole package to come together they also
need the car I designed.'

A small laugh burst from her lips. The sound was so unex-
pectedly pleasing he momentarily lost his train of thought, and
missed her reply.

'What did you say?'

'I said that's a clever strategy—considering you own the team
you design for, and the only other way anyone can get their hands
on a Marco de Cervantes design is by shelling out…how much
does the *Cervantes Conquistador* cost? Two million?'

'Three.'

She whistled—another unexpected sound that charged
through his bloodstream, making him even more on edge than
he'd been a handful of seconds ago.

She leaned forward into his eyeline. He'd been wrong about
the shirt being functional. Her pert breasts pressed against the
cotton material, her hands on her thighs as she peered down.

Marco swallowed, the hot stirrings in his abdomen increasing
to uncomfortable proportions. Ruthlessly he pushed them away.

Sasha Fleming was bad news, he reminded himself.

Rafael had got involved with her to his severe detriment.
Marco had no intention of following down the same road.
His only interest in her was to make sure she delivered the
Constructors' Championship. Now he knew what she really
wanted—the Drivers' Championship—he had her completely
at his mercy.

Control re-established, he brought the helicopter in to land,
and yanked off his headphones. Sasha jumped down without
his help and Marco caught the puzzled look she flashed him.
Ignoring it, he strode towards Luke Green. His chief engineer

had travelled ahead to supervise the initial training arrangements.

Sasha drew closer and her scent reached his nostrils. Marco's insides clenched in rejection even as he breathed her in. His awareness of her was becoming intolerable. Even her voice as she greeted Luke bit into his psyche.

'Is everything in order?' he asked.

Luke nodded. 'We're just about to offload the engine. The mechanics will check it over and make sure it hasn't been damaged during the flight.'

'It takes three hours max to assemble the car, so it should be ready for me to test this afternoon, shouldn't it?' Sasha asked, her attention so intent on the tarpaulin-covered engine Marco almost enquired if she yearned to caress it.

'No. You'll begin training tomorrow morning,' he all but growled.

Her head snapped towards him, her expression crestfallen. 'Oh, but if the car's here...'

'The mechanics have been working on getting things ready since dawn. This engine hasn't been used since last December. It'll have to go through rigorous testing before it's race-ready. That'll take most of the day—at least until sundown.'

He turned back to Luke. 'I want to see hourly engine readouts and a final telemetry report when you're done testing.'

'Sure thing, boss.'

Grabbing Sasha's arm, he steered her away from the garage. Several eyes followed them, but he didn't care. He was nothing like his brother. He had no intention of ever making a fool of himself over a woman again.

Opening the passenger door to his Conquistador, he thrust her into the bucket seat. Rounding the hood, he slid behind the wheel.

'Why do I get the feeling you're angry with me?' she directed at him.

Marco slammed his door. 'It's not a feeling.'

The breath she blew up disturbed the thick swathe of hair slanting over her forehead. 'What did I do?' she demanded.

He faced her and found her stunning eyes snapping fire at him. The blue of her gaze was so intense, so vivid, he wanted to keep staring at her for ever. The uncomfortable erotic heat he'd felt in her Budapest hotel room, when she'd strutted into view wearing that damned T-shirt that boldly announced *'Bite Me'*, rose again.

For days he'd been fighting that stupid recurring memory that strayed into his thoughts at the most inconvenient times.

Even here in Leon, where much more disturbing memories impinged everywhere he looked, he couldn't erase from his mind the sight of those long, coltish legs and the thought of how they would feel around his waist.

Nor could he ignore the evidence of Sasha's hard work and dedication to her career. Every night since her arrival in Spain he'd found her poring over telemetry reports or watching footage of past races, fully immersed in pursuing the only thing she cared about.

The only thing she cared about...

Grabbing the steering wheel, he forced himself to calm down. 'Marco?'

When had he given her permission to use his first name? Come to think of it, when had he started thinking of her as Sasha instead of Miss Fleming?

Dios, he was losing it.

With a wrench of his wrist the engine sprang to life, its throaty roar surprisingly soothing. Designing the Espiritu race cars had been an engineering challenge he'd relished. The *Cervantes Conquistador* had been a pure labour of love.

Momentarily he lost himself in the sounds of the engine, his mind picking up minute clicks and torsion controls. If he closed his eyes he would be able to imagine the aerodynamic flow of air over the chassis, visualise where each spark plug, each piston, nut and bolt was located.

But he didn't close his eyes. He kept his gaze fixed firmly ahead. His grip tightened around the wheel.

Her gaze stayed on him as he accelerated the green and black sports car out of the parking lot. The screech of tyres drew startled glances from the mechanics heading for the hangar. Marco didn't give a damn.

After a few minutes, when he felt sufficiently calm, he slowed down. 'It's not you.'

She didn't answer.

Shrugging, he indicated the rich forest surrounding them. 'It's this place.'

'This place? The race track or *Casa de Leon*?'

His jaw clenched as he tried in vain to stem the memories flooding him. 'This is where my mother died eight years ago.'

Her gasp echoed in the car. 'Oh, my God, I'm so sorry. I didn't know. You should've said something.'

He slowed down long enough to give her a hard look. 'It isn't common knowledge outside my family. I'd prefer it to remain that way.' He wasn't even sure why he'd told her. Whatever was causing him to act so out of character he needed to cauterise it.

She gave a swift nod. 'Of course. You can trust me.' Her colour rose slightly at her last words.

The irony wasn't lost on him. He only had himself to blame if she decided to spill her guts at the first opportunity. Flooring the accelerator, he sent the car surging forward as his *other* reason for wanting to escape the memories of this place rose.

Sasha remained silent until he pulled up in front of the villa. Then, lifting a hand, she tucked a strand of hair behind her ear. 'How did it happen?' she asked softly.

Releasing his clammy grip on the steering wheel, Marco flicked a glance at the villa door. He knew he'd find no respite within. If anything, the memories were more vivid inside. He didn't need to close his eyes to see his mother laughing at Rafael's shameless cajoling, her soft hazel eyes sparkling as she wiped her hands on a kitchen towel moments before rushing out of the villa.

'For his twenty-first birthday my father bought Rafael a Lamborghini. We celebrated at a nightclub in Barcelona. Afterwards I flew down here in the helicopter with my parents. Rafael chose to drive from Barcelona—five hours straight. He arrived just after breakfast, completely wired from partying. I tried to convince him to get some sleep, but he wanted to take my parents for a spin in the car.'

The familiar icy grip of pain tightened around his chest.

'Rafael was my mother's golden boy. He could do no wrong. So of course she agreed.' Marco felt some of the pain seep out and tried to contain it. 'My father insisted later it was the sun that got in Rafael's eyes as he turned the curve, but one eyewitness confirmed he took the corner too fast. I heard the crash from the garage.' Every excruciating second had felt like a lifetime as he sped towards the scene. 'By the time the air ambulance came my mother was gone.'

'Oh, Marco, *no!*'

Sasha's voice was a soft, soothing sound. The ache inside abated, but it didn't disappear. It never would. He'd lost his mother before he'd ever had the chance to make up for what he'd put her through.

'I should've stopped him—should've insisted he get some sleep before taking the car out again.'

'You couldn't have known.'

He shook his head. 'But I should have. Except when it comes to Rafael everyone seems to develop a blind spot. Including me.'

Vaguely, Marco wondered why he was spilling his guts. To Sasha Fleming, of all people. With a forceful wrench on the door, he stepped out of the car.

She scrambled out too. 'And your father? What happened to him?'

His fist tightened around the computerised car key. 'The accident severed his spine. He lost the use of his body from the neck down. He's confined to a wheelchair and will remain like that for the rest of his life.'

Sasha looked after Marco's disappearing figure, shocked by the astonishing revelation.

Now Marco's motives became clear. His overprotective attitude towards Rafael, his reaction to the crash, suddenly made sense. Watching his mother die on the race track *he'd* built had to be right up there with enduring a living hell every time he stepped foot on it.

So why did he do it?

Marco de Cervantes was an extraordinary engineer and aero-dynamicist, who excelled in building astonishingly fast race cars, but he could easily have walked away and concentrated his design efforts on the equally successful range of exclusive sport cars favoured by Arab sheikhs and Russian oligarchs.

So what drove him to have anything to do with a world that surely held heart-wrenching memories?

She slowly climbed the stairs and entered the house, her mind whirling as she went into her suite to wash off the heat and sweat of the race track.

After showering, she put on dark jeans and a striped blue shirt. Pulling her hair into a neat twist, she secured it with a band and shoved her feet into pair of flat sandals.

She met Marco as she came down the stairs. The now familiar raking gaze sent another shiver of awareness scything through her. He stopped directly in front of her, his arresting face and piercing regard rendering her speechless for several seconds.

'Lunch won't be ready for a while, but if you want something light before then, Rosario can fix you something.'

The matronly housekeeper appeared in the sun-dappled hallway as if by magic, wiping her hands on a white apron.

'No, thanks. I'm not hungry.'

With a glance, he dismissed the housekeeper. His gaze returned to her, slowly tracing her face. When it rested on her mouth she struggled not to run her tongue over it, remembering how his eyes had darkened the last time she'd done that.

'I have a video call with Tom Brooks, my press liaison, in five minutes. Can I use your study?'

His eyes locked on hers. 'Why's he calling?'

'He wants to go over next month's sponsorship schedule. I can give you a final printout, if you like.'

She deliberately kept her voice light, non-combative. Something told her Marco de Cervantes was spoiling for a fight, and after his revelations she wasn't sure it was wise to engage him in one. Pain had a habit of eroding rational thought.

Being calmly informed by the doctor that she'd lost the baby she hadn't even been aware she was carrying had made her want to scream—loudly, endlessly until her throat gave out. She'd wanted to reach inside herself and rip her body apart for letting her down. In the end the only thing that had helped was getting back to the familiar—to her racing car. The pain had never left her, but the adrenaline of racing had eased her aching soul the way nothing else had been able to.

Looking into Marco's dark eyes, she caught a glimpse of his pain, but wisely withheld the offer of comfort on the tip of her tongue. After all, who was *she* to offer comfort when she hadn't quite come to terms with losing her baby herself?

Silently, she held his gaze.

For several seconds he stared back. Then he indicated his study. 'I'll set it up for you.'

She followed him into the room and drew to a stunned halt. The space was so irreverently, unmistakably male that her eyes widened. An old-style burgundy leather studded chair and foot-rest stood before the largest fireplace she'd ever seen, above which two centuries-old swords hung. The rest of the room was oak-panelled, with dusty books stretching from floor to ceiling. The scent of stale tobacco pipe smoke hung in the air. It wouldn't have been strange to see a shaggy-haired professor seated be-hind the massive desk that stood under the only window in the room. Compared to the contemporary, exceedingly luxurious comfort of the rest of the villa, this was a throwback to another century—save for the sleek computer on the desk.

Marco caught the look on her face and raised an eyebrow as he activated the large flat screen computer on the immense mahogany desk.

'Did your designer fall into a time warp when he got to this room?'

'This was my father's study—his personal space. He never allowed my mother to redesign it, no matter how much she tried.

He hasn't been in here since she died, and I...I feel no need to change things.'

A well of sympathy rose inside Sasha for his pain. Casting a look around, she stopped, barely suppressing a gasp. 'Is that a stag's head on the wall?' she asked, eyeing the large animal head, complete with gnarled, menacing antlers.

'A bull stag, yes.'

She turned from the gruesome spectacle. 'There's a difference?'

The semblance of a smile whispered over his lips. Sasha found she couldn't tear her gaze away. In that split second she felt a wild, unfettered yearning to see that smile widen, to see his face light up in genuine amusement.

'The bull stag is the alpha of its herd. He calls the shots. And he gets his pick of the females.'

'Ah, I see. If you're going to display such a monstrosity on your wall, only the best will do?'

He slanted her a wry glance. 'That's the general thinking, yes.'

'Ugh.'

He caught her shudder and his smile widened.

Warmth exploded in her chest, encompassed her whole body and made her breathless. Sasha found she didn't care. The need to bask in the stunning warmth of his smile trumped the need for oxygen. Even when another voice intruded she couldn't look away.

When Tom's voice came again she roused herself with difficulty from the drugging race of her pulse, carefully skirted a coffee table festooned with piles of books, and approached the desk as the screen came to life.

'Hello? Can you hear me, Sasha?' Tom's voice held its usual touch of impatience, and his features were pinched.

Marco's smile disappeared.

Sasha mourned the loss of it and moved closer to the screen. 'I'm here, Tom.'

He huffed in response, then his eyes swung over her shoulder and widened.

'Sit down,' Marco said from behind her, pushing the massive chair towards her.

She sat. He reached over her shoulder and adjusted the screen. Then he remained behind her—a heavy, dominating presence.

Tom cleared his throat. 'Uh, I didn't know you'd be joining us, Mr de Cervantes.'

'A last-minute decision. Carry on,' Marco instructed.

'Um…okay…'

She'd never seen Tom flounder, and she bit the inside of her mouth to keep from smiling.

'Sasha, you have a Q&A on the team's website next Friday. I've e-mailed the questions to you. I'll need it back by Wednesday, to proofread and get it approved by the lawyers. On Friday night you have the Children of Bravery awards in London. Tuesday is the Strut footwear shoot, followed by the Linear Watches shoot in Barcelona. On Sun— Is there a problem?' he asked testily when she shook her head.

'That's not going to work. I can't take all that time off just for sponsorship events.'

'This is the schedule I've planned. You'll have to deal with it.'

'Seriously, I think it makes more sense to group everything together and get it done in the shortest possible time—'

'*I'm* in charge of your schedule. Let *me* work out what makes sense.'

'Miss Fleming is right.' Marco's deep voice sounded from behind her shoulder. 'You have several events spaced out over the period of a week. That's a lot of time wasted travelling. Do you not agree?'

'But the sponsors—'

'The sponsors need to work around her schedule, not the other way round. They can have Thursday to Saturday next week. Otherwise they'll have to wait until the end of the month. Miss Fleming gets Sundays off. Your job is to manage her time properly. Make it happen.'

Marco reached past Sasha and disconnected the link. Although it was a rare treat to see Tom get his comeuppance, a large part of her tightened with irritation.

'I'm perfectly capable of arranging my own schedule, thank you very much.'

'It didn't seem that way.'

'Only because you didn't give me half a chance.' She craned her neck to gaze up at him, feeling at a severe disadvantage.

His head went back as he glared down his arrogant nose at her. 'I didn't like the way he spoke to you,' he declared.

Her heart lurched, then swung into a dive as a wave of warmth oozed through her. Sasha berated herself for the foolish feeling, but as much as she tried to push it away it grew stronger.

Despite the alien feeling zinging through her, she tried for a casual shrug. 'I don't think he likes me very much.'

A frown creased his forehead. 'Why not?'

Her bitter laugh escaped before she could curb it. Rising, she padded several steps away, breathing easier. 'Probably for the same reasons you don't. He doesn't think I have any business being a racing driver. He believes I've made him a laughing stock by association.'

'Because of your gender or because of your past indiscretions?'

'According to you they're one and the same, aren't they?' she retorted.

The hands gripping the back of the chair tightened. 'I told you in Budapest your gender had nothing to do with my decision to fire you. Your talent as a full-time racing driver is yet to be seen. Prove yourself as the talented racing driver you claim to be and you'll earn your seat. Until then I reserve my judgement.'

'You reserve your judgement professionally, but you're judge, jury and executioner when it comes to my personal life?'

A cold gleam had entered his eyes, but even that didn't stop her from staring into those hypnotising depths.

'We agreed that you will have *no* personal life until your contract ends, did we not? You wouldn't be thinking of reneging on that agreement so soon, would you?'

Sasha just stopped herself from telling him she already had no personal life. That she hadn't had one since Derek's lies and the loss of her baby had put her through the wringer. Rafael had been her one and only friend until that had headed south.

'Sasha.'

The warning in the way he said her name sent a shiver dancing down her spine. She glanced up at him and bit back a gasp.

When had he drawn so close? Within his eyes she could see the flecks of green that spiked from his irises. And the lashes that framed them were long, silky. Beautiful. He had beautiful eyes. Eyes that drew her in, wove spells around her. Tugged at emotions buried deep within her...

Eyes that were steadily narrowing, demanding an answer.

She sucked in a breath, her brain turning fuzzy again when his scent—lemony, with a large dose of man—hit her nostrils. 'No, Marco. No personal life. Not even a Labradoodle to cuddle when I'm lonely.'

A frown deepened. 'A what?'

'It's a dog. A cross between a Labrador and a poodle. I used to have one when I was little. But it died.'

'Pets have no place on the racing circuit.'

She glared at him. 'I wasn't planning on bringing one to work. Anyway, it's a moot point, since my schedule isn't conducive to having one. I detest part-time pet owners.'

Her phone buzzed in her back pocket. She pulled it out and activated it. Seeing the promised e-mail from Tom, she turned to leave.

'Where are you going?' he demanded.

She faked a smile to hide the disturbing emotions roiling through her body. 'Oh, I thought the inquisition was over. Only Tom has sent the Q&A and I want to get it done so I don't take up valuable race testing time.'

Her snarky tone didn't go unmissed. His jaw clenched as he sauntered over to her. She held her breath, forcing herself not to move back.

'The inquisition is over for now. But I reserve the right to pursue it at a later date.'

'And *I* reserve the right not to participate in your little witch hunt. I read the small print and signed on the dotted line. I know exactly what's expected of me and I intend to honour our agreement. You can either let me get on with it, or you can impede me and cause us both a lot of grief. Your choice.'

She sailed out of the room, head held high. Just before the door swung shut Sasha suspected she heard a very low, very frustrated growl emitted by a very different bull stag from the one hanging on the wall.

Her smile widened as she punched the air.

Marco didn't come back for dinner. Even after Rosario told her he'd gone to his office in Barcelona Sasha caught herself looking towards the door, half expecting him to stride through it at any second.

Luke had dropped off the engine testing results, which she'd pored over half a dozen times in between listening out for the sound of the helicopter.

Catching herself doing so for the umpteenth time, she shoved away from the table, ran upstairs to her suite and changed into her gym clothes.

Letting herself out of the side entrance, she skirted the pool and jogged along the lamplit path bordering the extensive gardens. Fragrant bougainvillaea and amaranth scented the evening air. She breathed in deeply and increased her pace until she spotted the floodlights of the race track in the distance. Excitement fizzed through her veins.

A few hours from now she'd start her journey to clear her father's name. To prove to the world that the Fleming name was not dirt, as so many people claimed.

Fresh waves of sadness and anger buffeted her as she thought of her father. How his brilliant career had crumbled to dust in just a few short weeks, his hard work and sterling dedication to his team wiped away by vicious lies.

The pain of watching him spiral into depression had been excruciating. In the end even his pride in her hadn't been enough...

Whirling away from her thoughts, and literally from the path, she jogged the rest of the way to the sports facility half a mile

away and spent the next hour punishing herself through a stren-
uous routine that would have made Charlie, her physio, proud.

Leaving the gym, Sasha wandered aimlessly, deliberately
emptying her mind of sad memories. It wasn't until she nearly
stumbled into a wall that she realised she stood in front of a
single-storey building. Shrouded in darkness, it sat about half
a mile away from the house, at the far end of the driveway that
led past the villa.

About to enter, she jumped as the trill of her phone rang
through the silent night.

Hurriedly, she fished it out, but it went silent before she could
answer it. Frowning, she returned it to her pocket, then rubbed
her hands down her arms when the cooling breeze whispered
over her skin.

Casting another glance at the dark building, she retraced her
steps back to the villa. Her footsteps echoed on the marble floors.

'Where the hell have you been?'

Marco's voice was amplified in the semi-darkness, drawing
her to a startled halt. He stood half hidden behind one of the
numerous pillars in the vast hallway.

'I went to the gym, then went for a walk.'

His huge frame loomed larger as he came towards her. 'The
next time you decide to leave the house for a long stretch have
the courtesy to inform the staff of your whereabouts. That way
I won't have people combing the grounds for you.'

There was an odd inflection in his voice that made the hairs
on her neck stand up.

'Has something happened?' She stepped towards him, her
heart taking a dizzying dive when he didn't answer immediately. 'Marco?'

'*Sí*, something's happened,' he delivered in an odd, flat tone.

He stepped into the light and Sasha bit back a gasp at the
gaunt, tormented look on his face.

'Rafael… It's Rafael.'

CHAPTER FIVE

FEAR pierced through her heart but she refused to believe the worst. 'Is he…?' She swallowed and rephrased. 'How bad is it?'

Marco shoved his phone into his pocket and stalked down the hall towards the large formal sitting room. Set between two curved cast-iron balconies that overlooked the living room from the first-floor hallway, a beautifully carved, centuries-old drinks cabinet stood. Marco picked up a crystal decanter and raised an eyebrow. When she shook her head, he poured a healthy splash of cognac into a glass and threw it back in one quick swallow.

A fire had been lit in the two giant fireplaces in the room. Marco stood before one and raked a hand through his hair, throwing the dark locks into disarray. 'He's suffered another brain haemorrhage. They had to perform a minor operation to release the pressure. The doctors…' He shook his head, tightly suppressed emotion making his movements jerky. 'They can't do any more.'

'But the operation worked, didn't it?' She didn't know where the instinct to keep talking came from. All she knew was that Marco had come looking for her.

He sucked in a deep, shuddering breath. 'The bleeding has stopped, yes. And he's been put into an induced coma until the swelling goes down.'

She moved closer, her heart aching at the pain he tried to hide. 'That's good. It'll give him time to heal.'

His eyes grew bleaker. He looked around, as if searching for a distraction. 'I should be there,' he bit out. 'But the doctors think

I'm in their way.' He huffed. 'One even accused me of unreasonable behaviour, simply because I asked for a third opinion.'

The muttered imprecation that followed made Sasha bite her lip, feeling sorry for the unknown hapless doctor who'd dared clash with Marco.

She sucked in a breath as his gaze sharpened on her.

'Nothing to say?'

'He's your brother. You love him and want the best for him. That's why you've hired the best doctors to care for him. Maybe you need to leave them alone to do their jobs?' He looked set to bite her head off. 'And if he's in intensive care they probably need to keep his environment as sterile as possible. Surely you don't want anything to jeopardise his recovery?'

His scowl deepened and he looked away. 'I see you not only wear a psychologist's hat, you also dabble in diplomacy and being the voice of reason.'

Although Sasha did not enjoy his cynicism, she felt relieved that his voice was no longer racked with raw anguish. 'Yeah, that's me. Miss All-Things-To-All-People,' she joked.

Eyes that had moments ago held pain and anguish froze into solid, implacable ice. '*Sí*. Unfortunately that aspect of your nature hasn't worked out well for my brother, has it? Rafael needed you to be *one* thing to him. And you failed. *Miserably*.'

'I tried to talk some sense into him...'

Rafael hadn't taken it well when she'd pointed out the absurdity of his out-of-the-blue proposal. He'd stormed out of her hotel in Budapest the night before the race, and she'd never got the chance to talk to him before his accident.

Marco turned from the mantel and faced her. 'Don't tell me... You were *conveniently* unsuccessful?' he mocked.

'Because he didn't mean it.'

He pounced. 'Why would any man propose to a woman if he didn't mean it?'

When she didn't answer immediately, his scowl deepened. In the end, she said, 'Because of...other things he'd said.'

'What *other* things?' came the harsh rejoinder.

'*Private* things.' She wasn't about to deliver a blow-by-blow account. It wasn't her style. 'I thought he was reacting to his last break-up.'

He dismissed it with a wave of his hand. 'Rafael and Nadia broke up two months ago. Are you suggesting this was a re-bound?' Marco asked derisively. 'My brother's bounce-back rate is normally two *weeks*.'

Sasha frowned. 'Rafael's changed, Marco. To you he may have seemed like his normal wild, irreverent self. But—'

'Are you saying I don't know my own brother?' he demanded.

Slowly, Sasha shook her head. 'I'm just saying he may not have told you everything that was going on with him.'

Her breath caught at the derisive gleam that entered Marco's eyes.

'His text told me everything I needed to know. By refusing him, you gave him no choice but to come after you.'

'Of course I didn't!'

'Liar!'

'That's the second time you've called me a liar, Marco. For your own sake I hope there isn't a third. Or I'll take great plea-sure in slapping your face. Contract or no bloody contract. Whatever Rafael led you to believe, I *didn't* set out to ensnare him, or encourage him to fall for me—which I don't think he did, by the way. And I certainly didn't get him riled up enough to cause his accident. Whatever demons Rafael's been battling, they finally caught up with him. I'm tired of defending myself. I was just being his friend. Nothing else.'

Heart hammering, she took a seat on one of the extremely delicate-looking twin cream and gold striped sofas and pulled in a deep breath to steady the turbulent emotions coursing through her. Emotions she'd thought buckled down tight, but which Marco had seemed to spark to life so very easily.

'I find it hard to believe your actions have taken you down the same path twice in your life.'

'An unfortunate coincidence, but that's all it is. I have to live with it. However, I refuse to let you or anyone else label me some sort of *femme fatale*. All I want is to do my job.'

He sat down opposite her. When his gaze drifted down her

body, she struggled to fight the pinpricks of awareness he ignited along the way.

'You're a fighter. I admire that in you. There's also something about you...'

His pure Latin shrug held a wealth of expression that made her silently shake her head in awe.

'An unknown quality I find difficult to pinpoint. You're hardly a *femme fatale*, as you say. The uncaring way you dress, your brashness, all point to a lack of femininity—'

Pure feminine affront sparked a flame inside her. 'Thanks very much.'

'And normally I wouldn't even class you as Rafael's type. Yet on the night before his accident he was fiercely adamant that *you* were the one. Don't get me wrong, he's said that a few times in the past, but this time I knew something wasn't quite right.'

Despite his accusation, sympathy welled inside her. 'Did you two fight? Was that why you didn't come to Friday's practice?'

His nod held regret. 'I lost it when he asked for the ring.'

'You had it?'

He pinched the bridge of his nose and exhaled sharply. 'Yes. It belonged to our mother. She didn't leave it specifically to either of us; she just wanted the first one of us to get married to give it to his bride.' He shook his head once. 'I always knew it would go to Rafael since I never intend—' He stopped and drew in a breath. 'Rafael has claimed to be in love with many girls, but this was the first time he'd asked for the ring.'

'And you were angry because it was me?'

His jaw clenched. 'You could have waited until the race was over,' he accused, his voice rough with emotion.

'Marco—'

'He'd have had the August hiatus to get over you; he would've mended his broken heart in the usual way—ensconced on a yacht in St Tropez or chasing after some Hollywood starlet in LA. Either way, he would've arrived back on the circuit, smiled at you, and called you *pequeña* because he'd forgotten your name. Instead he's in a hospital bed, fighting for his life!'

'But I couldn't lie,' she shot back. 'He didn't want me—not

really. And I'm not on the market for a relationship. Certainly not after—' She pulled herself up short, but it was too late.

He stood and pulled her up, caught her shoulders in a firm grip. 'After what?'

'Not after my poor track record.'

'You mean what happened with your previous lover?'

She nodded reluctantly. 'Derek proposed just before I broke up with him. I'd known for some time that it wasn't working, but I convinced myself things would work out. When I declined his proposal a week later he accused me of leading him on. He said I was only refusing him because I wanted to sell myself to the highest bidder.'

Derek had repeated that assertion to every newspaper and team boss who would listen, and Sasha's career had almost ended because of it. She pushed the painful memories away.

'Rafael knew there was no way I'd get involved with him romantically.'

Marco's grip tightened, his gaze scouring her face as if he wanted to dig out the truth. Sasha forced herself to remain still, even though the touch of his hands on her branded her—so hot she wanted to scream with the incredibly forceful sensation of it.

'Do you know the last thing I said to him?' he rasped.

Her heart aching for him, she shook her head.

'I told him to stop messing around and grow up. That he was dishonouring our mother's memory by treating life like his own personal playground.' His eyelids veiled his gaze for several seconds and his jaw clenched, his emotions riding very near the surface. 'If anything happens to him—'

'It won't.'

Without thought, she placed her hand on his arm. Hard muscles flexed beneath her fingers. His eyes returned to her face, then dropped to her mouth. Sharp sensation shot through her belly, making her breath catch.

Sasha felt an electric current of awareness zing up her arm—a deeper manifestation of the intense awareness she felt whenever he was near. *Comfort*, she assured herself. *I'm offering him com-*

fort. That's all. This need to keep touching him was just a silly passing reaction.

'He'll wake up and he'll get better. You'll see.'

Face taut and eyes bleak, he slowly dropped his hands. 'I have to go,' he said.

She stepped back, her hands clenching into fists behind her back to conceal their trembling. 'You're returning to the hospital?'

He shook his head. 'I'm going to Madrid.'

Her belly clenched with the acute sense of loss. 'For how long?' she asked lightly.

'For however long it takes to reassure my father that his precious son isn't dying.'

The state-of-the-art crash helmet was no match for the baking North Spanish sun. Sasha sat in the cockpit of the Espiritu DSI, the car that had won Rafael the championship the year before. Eyes shut, she retraced the outline of the Belgian race track, anticipation straining through her.

Sweat trickled down her neck, despite the chute pumping cold air into the car. When she'd mentally completed a full circuit she opened her eyes.

They burned from lack of sleep, and she blinked several times to clear them. She'd been up since before dawn, the start of her restless night having oddly coincided with the moment Marco's helicopter had lifted off the helipad. For hours she'd lain tangled up in satin sheets, unable to dismiss the look on Marcus's anguished face from her mind. Or the heat of his touch on her body.

Firming her lips, she forcibly cleared her mind.

She wrapped fireproof gloved hands around the wheel and pictured the Double S bends at Eau Rouge, and the exact breaking point at La Source. Keeping her breathing steady, she finally achieved the mental calm she needed to block out the background noise of the mechanics and the garage. She emptied every thought from her mind, the turmoil of the past few days reduced to a small blot. She welcomed the relief of not having to dwell on anything except the promise of the fast track in front of her.

Her eyes remained steady on the mechanic's *STOP/GO* sign, her foot a whisper off the accelerator.

When the sign went up, she launched out of the garage onto the track. Adrenalin coursed through her veins as the powerful car vibrated beneath her. Braking into the first corner, she felt G-forces wrench her head to the left and smiled. This battle with the laws of physics lent an extra thrill as she flew along the track, the sense of freedom making her oblivious to the stress on her body as lap after lap whizzed by.

'You're being too hard on your tyres, Sasha.'

Luke's voice piped into her earphones and she immediately adjusted the balance of the car, her grip loosening a touch to help manoeuvre the curves better.

'That's better. In race conditions you'll need them to go for at least fifteen laps. You can't afford to wear them out in just eight. It's early days yet, but things look good.'

Sasha blinked at the grudging respect in Luke's voice.

'How does the car feel?'

'Er…great. It feels great.'

'Good. Come in and we'll take a look at the lap times together.'

She drove back into the garage and parked. Keeping her focus on Luke as he approached her, she got out and set her helmet aside.

He showed her the printout. 'We can't compare it with the performance of the DSII, but from these figures things are looking very good for Spa in three weeks' time.'

Reading through the data, Sasha felt a buzz of excitement. 'The DSII is great at slow corners, so I should be able to go even faster.'

Luke grinned. 'When you have the world's best aerodynamicist as your boss, you have a starting advantage. We'll have a battle on the straight sections, but if you keep up this performance we should cope well enough to keep ourselves ahead.'

Again she caught the changed note in his voice.

Although she'd tried not to dwell on it, throughout the day, and over the following days during testing, Sasha slowly felt the changing attitude of her small team. They spoke to her with less condescension; some even bothered to engage her in conversation before and after her practice sessions.

And the first time Luke asked her opinion on how to avoid the under steering problem that had cropped up, Sasha forced herself to blink back the stupid tears that threatened.

Marco heard the car drive away as he came down the stairs. He curbed the strong urge to yank the door open and forced himself to wait. When he reached the bottom step he sat down and rested his elbows on his knees, his BlackBerry dangling from his fingers.

Light footsteps sounded seconds before the front door opened.

Sasha stood silhouetted against the lights flooding the outer courtyard, the outline of her body in tight dark trousers and top making sparks of desire shoot through his belly.

Clenching his teeth against the intensity of it, he forced himself to remain seated, knowing she hadn't yet spotted him in the darkened hallway. Her light wrap slipped as she turned to shut the door, and he caught a glimpse of one smooth shoulder and arm. Her dark silky hair was tied in a careless knot on top of her head, giving her neck a long, smooth, elegant line that he couldn't help but follow.

He found himself tracing the lines of her body, wondering how he'd ever thought her boyish. She was tall, her figure lithe, but there were curves he hadn't noticed before—right down to the shapely denim-clad legs.

Shutting the door, she tugged off her boots and kicked them into a corner.

She turned and stumbled to a halt, her breath squeaking out in alarm. 'Marco! Damn it, you *really* need to stop skulking in dark hallways. You nearly scared me to death!'

'I wasn't skulking.' He heard the irritation in his voice and forced himself to calm down. 'Where have you been? I called you several times.'

She pulled the wrap tighter around her shoulders, her chin tilting up in silent challenge. 'I went for a drink with the team.

They're all flying out tomorrow morning and I wanted to say goodbye. I know that wasn't part of the deal—me socialising with the team—but they kept asking and it would have been surly to refuse.'

Annoyance rattled through him. The last thing he wanted to discuss was his team, or the deal he'd made with Sasha Fleming. *Dios*, he wasn't even sure why he'd come back here. He should be by his brother's bedside—even if the doctors intended to keep him in his induced coma until the swelling on his brain reduced.

'And you were having such a great time you decided not to answer your phone?'

'I think it's died.'

'You *think*?'

'You're annoyed with me. Why?'

Sasha asked the question in that direct way he'd come to expect from her. No one in his vast global organisation would dare to speak to him that way. And yet...he found he liked it.

Rising, he walked towards her. A few steps away, the scent of her perfume hit his nostrils. Marco found himself craving more of it, wanting to draw even closer. 'Why bother with a phone if you can't ensure it works?'

'Because no one calls me.'

Her words stopped him in his tracks. For a man who commanded his multi-billion-euro empire using his BlackBerry, Marco found her remark astonishing in the extreme. 'No one calls you?'

'My phone never rings. I think *you* were the last person to call me. I get the occasional text from Tom, or Charlie, my physio, but other than that...zilch.'

Marco's puzzlement grew. 'You don't have any friends?'

'Obviously none who care enough to call. And, before you go feeling sorry for me, I'm fine with it.'

'You're fine with being lonely?'

'With being *alone*. There's a difference. So, is there another reason you're annoyed with me?'

She raised her chin in that defiant way that drew his gaze to her throat.

He shoved his phone into his pocket. 'I'm not annoyed. I'm tired. And hungry. Rosario had gone to bed when I arrived.'

'Oh, well, that's good. Not the tired and hungry part. The not annoyed part.' She bit her lip, her eyes wide on his as he moved even closer. 'And about Rosario…I hope you don't mind, but I told her not to wait up for me.'

Marco shook his head. 'So where did you go for this drink?' He strove to keep his voice casual.

'A bodega just off Plaza Mayor in Salamanca.'

He nodded, itching to brush back the stray hair that had fallen against her temple. 'And did you enjoy your evening out?'

Her shrug drew his eyes to her bare shoulder. 'Leon is beautiful. And I was glad to get out of the villa.'

Her response struck a strangely discordant chord within him. 'You don't like it here?'

'I don't mind the proximity to the track, but I was tired of knocking about in this place all by myself.'

Marco stiffened. 'Do you want to move to the hotel with the rest of the team?'

She thought about it. Then, 'No. The crew and I seem to be gelling, but I don't want to become overly familiar with them.'

Marco found himself breathing again. 'Wise decision. Sometimes maintaining distance is the only way to get ahead.'

'*You* obviously don't practise that dogma. You're always surrounded by an adoring crowd.'

'X1 Premier Racing is a multi-million-spectator sport. I can't exist in a vacuum.'

'Okay. Um…do you think we can turn the lights on in here? Only we seem to be making a habit of having conversations in the dark.'

'Sometimes comfort can be found in darkness.'

Facing up to reality's harsh light after his own crash ten years ago had made him wish he'd stayed unconscious. Angelique's smug expression as she'd dropped her bombshell had certainly made him wish for the oblivion of darkness.

Sasha gave a light, musical laugh. The sound sent tingles of pleasure down his spine even as heat pooled in his groin. His eyes fell to her lips and Marco experienced the supreme urge to kiss her. Or to keep enjoying the sound of her laughter.

'What's so funny?' he asked as she reached over his shoulder and flipped on the light switch.

'I was thinking either you're very hungry or you're very tired, because you've gone all cryptic on me.'

He *was* hungry. And not just for food. A hunger—clawing and extremely ravenous—had taken hold inside him.

Pushing aside the need to examine it, he followed her as she headed towards the kitchen. The sight of her bare feet on the cool stones made his blood thrum faster as he studied her walk, the curve of her full, rounded bottom.

'I could do with a snack myself. Do you want me to fix you something?'

Walking on the balls of her feet made the sway of her hips different, sexier. He tried to stop himself staring. He failed.

'You cook?' he asked past the strain in his throat.

'Yep. Living on my own meant I had to learn, starve or live on takeaways. Starving was a bore, and Charlie would've had conniptions if he'd seen me within a mile of a takeaway joint. So I took an intensive cookery course two years ago.'

She folded her wrap and placed it on the counter, along with a small handbag. Only then did he see that her top was held up by the thinnest of straps.

Opening the fridge, she began to pull out ingredients. 'Roast beef sandwich okay? Or if you want something hot I can make pasta carbonara?' she asked over her shoulder.

Marco pulled up a seat at the counter, unable to take his eyes off her. 'I'm fine with the sandwich.'

Her nod dislodged more silky hair from the knot on her head. 'Okay.' Long, luxurious tresses slipped down to caress her neck.

She moved around the kitchen, her movements quick, efficient. In less than five minutes she'd set a loaded plate and a bottle of mineral water before him. He took a bite, chewed.

'This is really good.'

Her look of pleasure sent another bolt of heat through him.

He waited until she sat opposite him before taking another bite. 'So, how long have you lived on your own?'

'Since…' She hesitated. 'Since my father died four years ago.'

She looked away, but not before he caught shadows of pain within the blue depths.

'And your mother? Is she not around?'

She shook her head and picked up her sandwich. 'She died when I was ten. After that it was just Dad and me.'

The sharp pain of losing his own mother surfaced. Ruthlessly, he pushed it away.

'The team are wondering how Rafael is,' Sasha said, drawing him away from his disturbing thoughts.

'Just the team?'

She shrugged. 'We're all concerned.'

'Yes, I know. His condition hasn't changed. I've updated Russell. He'll pass it on to the team.'

He didn't want to talk about his brother. Because speaking of Rafael would only remind him of why this woman who made the best sandwich he'd ever tasted was sitting in front of him.

'How is your father holding up?'

He didn't want to talk about his father either.

Recalling his father's desolation, Marco shoved away his plate. 'He watched his son crash on live TV. How do you think he's doing?'

A flash of concern darkened her blue eyes. 'Does he…does he know about me?' she asked in a small voice.

'Does he know the cause of his son's crash is the same person taking his seat?' He laughed. 'Not yet.'

He wasn't sure why he'd kept that information from his father. It certainly had nothing to do with wondering if his brother's version of events was completely accurate, despite Rafael's voice ringing in his head… *She's the one, Marco.*

Sasha's gaze sought his, the look into them almost imploring. 'I didn't cause him to crash, Marco.'

Frustrated anger seared his chest. 'Didn't you?'

She shook her head and the knot finally gave up its fight. Dark, silky tresses cascaded over her naked shoulders and everything inside Marco tightened. It was the first time he'd seen it down, and despite the fury rolling through him the sudden urge to sink his fingers into the glossy mass, feel its decadent luxury, surged like fire through his veins.

'Then what did? Something must have happened to make him imagine that idiotic move would stick.'

Her lips pursed. The look in her eyes was reluctant. Then she sighed. 'I saw him just before the race. He was arguing with Raven.'

Marco frowned. 'Raven Blass? His physio?'

She nodded. 'I tried to approach him but he walked away. I thought I'd leave him to cool off and talk to him again after the race.'

Marco's muttered expletive made her brows rise, but he was past caring. He strode into the alcove that held his extensive wine collection. 'I need a drink. White or red?'

'I shouldn't. I had a beer earlier.' She tucked a silky strand behind one ear.

Watching the movement, he found several incredibly unwise ideas crowding his brain. Reaching out, he grabbed the nearest bottle. 'I don't like drinking alone. Have one with me.'

Her smile caused the gut-clenching knot to tighten further. 'Is the great Marco de Cervantes admitting a flaw?'

'He's admitting that his brother drives him *loco*.' He grabbed two crystal goblets.

'Fine. I was going to add another twenty minutes to my workout regime to balance out the incredible *tapas* I had earlier. I'll make it an even half-hour.'

Marco's gaze glided over her. 'You're hardly in bad shape.'

Another sweet, feminine laugh tumbled from her lips, sparking off a frenzied yearning.

'Charlie would disagree with you. Apparently my body mass index is *way* below acceptable levels.'

Marco uncorked the wine, thinking perhaps Charlie needed his eyes examined. 'How long is your daily regime?'

'Technically three hours, but Charlie keeps me at it until I'm either screaming in agony or about to pass out. He normally stops once I'm thoroughly dripping in sweat.'

His whole body froze, arrested by the image of a sweat-soaked Sasha, with sunshine glinting off her toned body.

Dios, this was getting ridiculous. He should not be feeling like this—especially not towards the woman who was the every epitome of Angelique: ruthlessly ambitious, uncaring of anything that got in her way. Sasha had nearly destroyed his brother the way Angelique had destroyed Marco's desire ever to forge a lasting relationship.

And yet in Barcelona he'd found himself thinking of Sasha... admitting to himself that his sudden preoccupation with her had nothing to do with work. And everything to do with the woman herself. The attraction he'd felt in Budapest was still present... and escalating.

Which was totally unacceptable.

He took a deep breath and wrenched control back into his body. While his brother was lying in a coma, the only thing he needed to focus on was winning the Constructors' Championship. And teaching Sasha Fleming a lesson.

He poured bold red Château Neuf into one glass and set it in front of her. 'I've seen the testing reports. You'll need to find another three-tenths of a second around Eau Rouge to give yourself a decent chance or you'll leave yourself open to overtaking. Belgium is a tough circuit.'

She took a sip and his gaze slid to the feline-like curve of her neck. Clenching fingers that itched to touch, he sat down opposite her.

'The DSII will handle the corners better.'

His eyes flicked over her face, noting her calm. 'You don't seem nervous.'

Another laugh. A further tightening in his groin.

Madre di Dios. It had been a while since he'd indulged in good, old-fashioned, no-holds-barred sex. Sexual frustration had a habit of making the unsavoury tempting, but this...this yearning was insane.

Mentally, he scanned through his electronic black book and

came up with several names. Just as fast he discarded every one of them, weariness at having to disentangle himself from expectation dampening his urge to revisit old ground.

Frustration built, adding another strand of displeasure to his already seething emotions.

'Believe me, I get just as nervous as the next racer. But I don't mind.'

'Because winning is everything, no matter the cost?' he bit out.

Her eyes darkened. 'No. Because nerves serve a good purpose. They remind you you're human; they sharpen your focus. I'd be terrified if I wasn't nervous. But eighteen years of experience also helps. I've been doing this since I was seven years old. Having a supportive father who blatantly disregarded the fact that I wasn't a boy helped with my confidence too.'

'Not a lot of parents agree with their children racing. You were lucky.'

She smiled. 'More like pushy. I threw a tantrum every time he threatened to leave me with my nanny. I won eventually. Although I get the feeling he was testing me to see how much I wanted it.'

'And you passed with flying colours.' He raised his glass to her. 'Bravo.'

Unsettlingly perceptive blue eyes rested on him. 'Oops, do I detect a certain cynicism there, Marco?'

He clenched his teeth as his control slipped another notch. 'Has anyone told you it's not nice to always go for the jugular?'

Her eyes widened. 'Was that what I was doing? I thought we were having a get-to-know-each-other conversation. At least until you went a little weird on me.'

'*Perdón.* Weird wasn't what I was aiming for.' He took a large gulp of his wine.

'First an admission of a flaw. Now an apology. Wow—must be my lucky night. Are you feeling okay? Maybe it would help to talk about whatever it is that spooked you?'

Perhaps it was the mellowing effect of the wine. Perhaps it was the fact that he hadn't had an engaging conversation like this in a while. Marco was surprised when he found himself laughing.

'I have no memory of ever being spooked. But, just for curiosity's sake, which hat will you be wearing for this little heart-to-heart? Diplomat or psychologist?'

Her gaze met his squarely. 'How about friend?' she asked.

His laughter dried up.

She wanted to be his friend.

Marco couldn't remember the last time anyone had offered to be his friend. Betrayal had a habit of stripping the scales from one's eyes. He'd learnt that lesson well and thoroughly.

He swallowed another gulp of wine. 'I respectfully decline. Thanks all the same.'

A small smile curved her lip. 'Ouch. At least you didn't laugh in my face.'

'That would have been cruel.'

One smooth brow rose. 'And you don't do cruel? You've come very close in the past.'

'You were a threat to my brother.'

'*Were?* You mean you're not under that impression any more?'

Realising the slip, he started to set her straight, then paused. *You can't control what happens in life...Rafael will resent you for controlling his life...* 'I'm willing to suspend my judgement until Rafael is able to set the picture straight himself.'

Her smile faded. 'You don't trust me at all, do you?'

He steeled himself against his fleeting tinge of regret at the hurt in her voice.

'Trust is earned. It comes with time. Or so I'm told.'

So far no one had withstood the test long enough for Marco to verify that belief. Sasha Fleming had already failed that test. She was only sitting across from him because of what he could give her.

She hid her calculating nature well, but he knew it was there, hiding beneath the fiercely determined light in her eyes.

'Well, then, here's to earning trust. And becoming friends.'

Marco didn't respond to her toast because part of him regretted the fact that friendship between them would never be possible.

CHAPTER SIX

'THIS way, Sasha!'

'Over here!'

'Smile!'

The Children of Bravery awards took place every August at one of the plushest hotels in Mayfair. Last year Sasha had arrived in a cab with Tom, who had then gone on to ignore her for the rest of the night.

Tonight flashbulbs went off in her face the moment Marco helped her out of the back of his stunning silver Rolls-Royce onto the red carpet.

Blinking several times to help her eyes adjust, she found Tom had materialised beside her. Before he could speak, Marco stepped in front of him.

'Miss Fleming won't be needing you tonight. Enjoy your evening.'

The dismissal was softly spoken, wrapped in steel. With a hasty nod, a slightly pale Tom dissolved back into the crowd.

'That wasn't very nice,' she murmured, although secretly she was pleased. Her nerves, already wound tight at the thought of the evening ahead, didn't need further negative stimulus in the form of Tom. 'But thank you.'

'De nada,' he murmured in that smooth deep voice of his, and her nerves stretched a little tighter.

When he took her arm the feeling intensified, then morphed into a different kind of warmth as another sensation altogether enveloped her—one of feeling protected, cherished...

She applied mental brakes as her brain threatened to go into meltdown. Forcing herself away from thoughts she had no business thinking, she drew in a shaky breath and tried to project a calm, poised demeanour.

'For once I agree with the paparazzi. *Smile.* Your face looks frozen,' Marco drawled, completely at ease with being the subject of intense scrutiny.

He seemed perfectly okay with hundreds of adoring female fans screaming his name from behind the barriers, while she could only think about the ceremony ahead and the memories it would resurrect.

Pushing back her pain, she forced her lips apart. 'That's probably because it is. Besides, you're one to talk. I don't see you smiling.'

One tuxedo-clad shoulder lifted in a shrug. 'I'm not the star on show.' He peered closer at her. 'What's wrong with you? You didn't say a word on the way over here and now you look pale.'

'That's because I don't *like* being on show. I hate dressing up, and make-up makes my face feel weird.'

'You look fine.' His gaze swept over her. 'More than fine. The stylist chose well.'

'She didn't choose this dress. I chose it myself. If I'd gone with her choice I'd be half naked with a slit up to my cro—' She cleared her throat. 'Why did you send me a stylist anyway?'

When she'd opened the door to Marco's Kensington penthouse apartment to find a stylist with a rack of designer gear in tow, Sasha had been seriously miffed.

'I didn't want to risk you turning up here in baggy jeans and a hippy top.'

'I'd never have—!' She caught the gleam of amusement in his eyes and relaxed.

Another photographer screamed her name and she tensed.

'Relax. *You* chose well.' His gaze slid over her once more. 'You look beautiful.'

Stunned, she mumbled, 'Thank you.'

She smoothed a nervous hand over her dress, thankful her new contract had come with a lucrative remuneration package that meant she'd been able to afford the black silk and lace floor-length Zang Toi gown she wore.

The silver studs in the off-the-shoulder form-fitting design flashed as the cameras went off. But even the stylish dress, with its reams of material that trailed on the red carpet, couldn't stem the butterflies ripping her stomach to shreds as the media screamed out for even more poses. Nor could it eliminate the wrenching reason why, on a night like this, she couldn't summon a smile.

'Stop fidgeting,' he commanded.

'That's easy for you to say. Anyway, why are you here? I don't need a keeper.' Nor did she need the stupid melting sensation in her stomach every time his hand tightened around her arm.

'I beg to differ. This event is hosting many sport personalities, including other drivers from the circuit. Your track record— pardon the pun—doesn't stand you in good stead. The one thing you *do* need is a keeper.'

'And you're it? Don't you have better things to do?'

When he'd pointed out after they'd landed this morning that it was more time-efficient for her to stay with him in London, than to come to the ceremony from her cottage in Kent, she hadn't bargained on the fact that he'd appoint himself her personal escort for the evening.

His rugged good looks lit up in sharp relief, courtesy of another photographer's flash, but he hardly noticed how avidly the media craved his attention. Nor cared.

'The team has suffered with Rafael's absence. It'll be good for the sponsors to see me here.'

The warmth she'd experienced moments ago disappeared. She felt his sharp gaze as she eased her arm from his grasp.

'How long do we have to stay out here?' The limelight was definitely a place she wasn't comfortable in. However irrational, she always feared her deepest secret would be exposed.

'Until a problem with the seating is sorted out.'

She swivelled towards him. 'What problem with the seating?'

Relief poured through her as he steered her away from the

cameras and down the red carpet into the huge marble-floored foyer of the five-star hotel.

The crowd seemed to pause, both men and women alike staring avidly as they entered.

Oblivious to the reaction, Marco snagged two glasses of champagne and handed one to her. 'Some wires got crossed along the line.'

Sasha should have been used to it by now, but a hard lump formed in her throat nonetheless. 'You mean I was downgraded to nobody-class because my surname is Fleming and not de Cervantes?'

He gave her a puzzled look. 'Why should your name matter?'

'Come on. I may have missed school the day rocket science was taught, but I know how this works.' Even when the words weren't said, Sasha knew she was being judged by her father's dishonour.

'Your surname has nothing to do with it,' Marco answered, nodding greetings to several people who tried to catch his eye. 'When the awards committee learned I would be attending, they naturally assumed that I would be bringing a plus one.'

A sensation she intensely disliked wormed its way into her heart. 'Oh, so I was bumped to make room for your date. Not because…?'

He raised a brow. 'Because?'

Shaking her head, Sasha took a hasty sip of her bubbly. 'So why didn't you? Bring a date, I mean?' When his brow rose in mocking query, she hurried on. 'I know it's certainly not for the lack of willing companions. I mean, a man like you…' She stumbled to a halt.

'A man like me? You mean The Ass?' he asked mockingly.

Heat climbed into her cheeks but she refused to be cowed. 'No, I didn't mean that. The other you—the impossibly rich, successful one, who's a bit decent to look at….' Cursing her runaway tongue, she clamped her mouth shut.

'*Gracias*…I think.'

'You know what I mean. Women scale skylights, risk life and limb to be with you, for goodness' sake.'

'Skylight-scaling is a bit too OTT for me. I prefer my women to use the front door. *With* my invitation.' His gaze connected with hers.

Heat blazed through her, lighting fires that had no business being lit. His broad shoulders loomed before her as he bent his head. As if to... As if to... Her gaze dropped to his lips. She swallowed.

Chilled champagne went down the wrong way.

She coughed, cleared her throat and tried desperately to find something to say to dispel the suddenly charged atmosphere. His eyelids descended, but not before she caught a flash of anguish. Stunned, she stared at him, but when he looked back up his expression was clear.

'To answer your question, this is a special event to honour children. It's not an event to bring a date who'll spend all evening checking out other women's jewellery or celebrity-spotting.'

'How incredibly shallow! Oh, I don't mean you date shallow women—I mean... Hell, I've put my foot in it, haven't I?'

The smile she'd glimpsed once before threatened to break the surface of his rigid demeanour. 'Your diplomatic hat is slipping, Sasha. I think we should go in before you insult me some more and completely shatter my ego.'

'I don't think that's possible,' she murmured under her breath. 'Seriously, though, you should smile more. You look almost human when you do.'

The return of his low, deep laugh sang deliciously along her skin, then wormed its way into her heart. When his hand arrived in the small of her back to steer her into the ballroom a whole heap of pleasure stole through her, almost convincing her the butterflies had been vanquished.

The feeling was pathetically short-lived. The pictures of children hanging from the ceiling of the chandeliered ballroom punched a hole through the euphoric warmth she'd dared to bask in. Her breath caught as pain ripped through her. If her baby had lived she would have been four by now.

'Are you sure you're okay?' Marco demanded in a low undertone.

'Yes, I'm fine.'

Unwilling to risk his incisive gaze, she hurried to their table and greeted an ex-footballer who'd recently been knighted for his work with children.

Breathing through her pain, it took a moment for her to realise she was the subject of daggered looks and whispered sniggers from the other two occupants of the table.

Feeling her insides congeal with familiar anger, she summoned a smile and pasted it on her face as the ex-footballer's trophy wife leaned forward, exposing enough cleavage to sink a battleship.

'Hi, I'm Lisa. This is my sister, Sophia,' she said.

Marco nodded in greeting and introduced Sasha.

Sophia flashed Marco a man-gobbling smile, barely sparing Sasha a glance.

A different form of sickness assailed Sasha as she watched the women melt under Marco's dazzling charisma. Eager eyes took in his commanding physique, the hard beauty of his face, the sensual mouth and the air of authority and power that cloaked him.

He murmured something that made Sophia giggle with delight. When her gaze met Sasha's, it held a touch of triumph that made Sasha want to reach out and pull out her fake hair extensions. Instead she kept her smile and turned towards the older man.

If fake boobs and faker lashes were his thing, Marco was welcome to them.

Marco clenched his fist on his thigh and forced himself to calm down. He'd never been so thoroughly and utterly ignored by a date in his life.

So Sasha wasn't technically his date. So what? She'd arrived with him. She would leave with him. Would it hurt her to try and make conversation with *him* instead of engaging in an indepth discussion of the current Premier League?

Slowly unclenching his fist, he picked up his wine glass.

Sasha laughed. The whole table seemed to pause to drink it in—even the two women who had so rudely ignored her so far.

By the time the tables were cleared of their dinner plates he'd had enough.

'Sasha.'

She smiled an excuse at the older man before turning to him. 'Yes?'

At the sight of her wide, genuine smile—the same one she'd worn when she'd offered her friendship at *Casa de Leon*—something in his chest contracted. He forced himself to remember the reason Sasha Fleming was here beside him. Why she was in his life at all.

Rafael. The baby brother he'd always taken care of.

But he isn't a child any more...

Marco suppressed the unsettling voice. 'The ceremony's about to start. You're presenting the second award.'

Her eyes widened a fraction, then anxiety darkened their depths.

'Yes, of course. I...I have my speech ready. I'd better read it over one more time, just in case...' Her hands shook as she plucked a tiny piece of paper from her bag.

Without thinking, he covered her hand with his. 'Take a deep breath. You'll be fine.'

Eyes locked onto his, she slowly nodded. 'I... Thanks.'

The MC took to the stage and announced the first award-giver. Sasha smiled and clapped but, watching her closely, Marco caught a glimpse of the pain in her eyes. Forcing himself to concentrate on the speech, he listened to the story of a four-year-old who'd saved her mother's life by ringing for an ambulance and giving clear, accurate directions after her mother had fallen down a ravine.

The ice-cold tightening his chest since he'd stepped from the car increased as he watched the little girl bound onto the stage in a bright blue outfit, her face wreathed in smiles. Forcing himself not to go there, not to dwell in the past, he turned to gauge Sasha's reaction.

She was frozen, her whole body held taut.

Frowning, he leaned towards her. 'This is ridiculous. Tell me what's wrong. *Now.*'

She jumped, her eyes wide, darkly haunted with unshed tears. Her smile flashed, only this time it lacked warmth or substance.

'I told you, I'm fine. Or I would if I'd remembered to bring a tissue.'

Wordlessly, he reached into his tuxedo jacket and handed her his handkerchief, a million questions firing in his mind.

Accepting it, she dabbed at her eyes. 'If I look a horror, don't tell me until I come back from the stage, okay?' she implored.

It was on the tip of his tongue to trip out the usual platitudes he gave to his dates. Instead he nodded. 'Agreed.'

Marco watched her gather herself together. A subtle roll of her shoulders and a look of determination settled over her features. By the time she rose to present the award her smile was fixed in place.

Watching the lights play over her dark hair, illuminate her beautiful features and the generous curve of her breasts, Marco felt the familiar tightening in his groin and bit back a growl of frustration.

'As most of you know, Rafael de Cervantes was supposed to present this award to Toby this evening. Instead he's skiving off somewhere in sunny Spain.'

Laughter echoed through the room.

'No, seriously, just as Toby said a prayer before rushing into his burning home to save his little sister and brother, so we should all take a moment to say a prayer for Rafael's speedy recovery. Toby fought for his family to live. Not once did he give up. Even when the rescuers told him there was no hope for his little brother he ignored them and rescued him. Why? Because he'd promised his mother he'd take care of his siblings. And he never once wavered from that promise. There are lessons for all of us in Toby's story. And that's never to give up. No matter how small or big your dreams, no matter how tough or impossible the way forward seems, never give up. I'm delighted to present this award to Toby Latham, for his outstanding bravery against all odds.'

Sasha's voice broke on the last words. Although she tried to hide it, Marco caught the strain in her face and the pain behind her smile even as thunderous applause broke out in the ballroom.

Automatically Marco followed suit, but inside ice clenched his heart, squeezing until he couldn't breathe. It was always like this when he allowed himself to remember what Angelique had taken from him. What his weakness had cost him. He'd failed to take care of his own.

Never again, he vowed silently.

Sasha stepped down from the stage and made her way back to her seat. Despite the rushing surge of memories, he couldn't take his eyes off her. In fact he wanted to jump up, grab her hand and lead her away from the ballroom.

She reached the table and smiled at him. 'Thank God I didn't fall on my face.'

Sliding gracefully into the seat, she tucked her hair behind one ear. In that moment Marco, struggling to breathe and damning himself to hell, knew he craved her.

Impossibly. Desperately.

Sasha caught the expression on Marco's face and her heart stopped.

'What's the matter? Oh, my God, if you tell me I have food caught in my teeth I'll kill you!' she vowed feverishly.

Desperately blinking back the threatening tears, she tried to stem the painful memories that looking into Toby Latham's face had brought. She couldn't afford to let Marco see her pain. The pain she'd let eat her alive, consume her for years, but had never been able to put to rest.

She heard sniggers from across the table but ignored them, her attention held hostage by the savagely intense look in Marco's eyes.

'Your teeth are fine,' he replied in a deep, rough voice.

'Then what? Was my speech that bad?' Caught in the traumatising resurgence of painful memories, she'd discarded her carefully prepared notes and winged it.

'No. Your speech was…*perfecto*.'

Her heart lurched at his small pause. Before she could question him about it the MC introduced the next guest. With no choice but to maintain a respectful silence, she folded her shaking hands in her lap.

Frantically, she tried to recall her speech word for word. Marco was obviously reacting to something she'd said. Had she been wrong to mention Rafael? Had her joke been too crass? A wave of shame engulfed her at the thought.

She waited until the next award had been presented, then leaned over. 'I'm sorry,' she whispered into his ear.

His head swivelled towards her. His jaw brushed her cheek, sending a thousand tiny electric currents racing through her.

'What for?' he asked.

'I shouldn't have made that crack about Rafael skiving off. It was tasteless—'

'And exactly what Rafael himself would've done had the situation been reversed. Everyone's been skirting around the subject, either pretending it's not happening or treating it with kid gloves. You gave people the freedom to acknowledge what had happened and set them at ease. I'm no longer the object of pitying glances and whispered speculation. It is I who should be thanking you.'

'Really?'

'Sí,' he affirmed, his gaze dropping to her mouth.

'Then why did you look so…*off*?'

His eyes darkened. 'Your words were powerful. I was touched. I'm not made of stone, Sasha, contrary to what you might think.'

The reproach in his voice shamed her.

'Oh, I'm sorry. It's just… I thought…'

'Forget it.'

He gave a tight smile, turned away and addressed Sophia, who flashed even more of her cleavage in triumph.

As soon as the last award was given, Sophia turned to Marco. 'We're going clubbing.' She named an exclusive club frequented by young royals. 'We'd love you to join us, Marco,' she gushed.

Sasha gritted her teeth but stayed silent. If Marco wanted

to party with the Fake Sisters it was his choice. All the same, Sasha held her breath as she waited for his answer, hating herself as she did so.

'Clubbing isn't my scene, but thanks for the offer.'

'Oh, we don't have to go clubbing. Maybe we can do something…*else*?'

Sasha stood and walked away before she could hear Marco's response.

She'd almost reached the ballroom doors when she felt his presence beside her. The wave of relief that flooded her body threatened to weaken her knees. Sternly, she reminded herself that Marco's presence had nothing to do with her personally. He was here for the team's sake.

'Are you sure you'd rather not be out with the Fa… Sophia? She seemed very eager to show you a good time. Seriously, I can take a taxi back.'

His limo pulled up. He handed her inside, then slid in beside her. 'I prefer to end my evening silicone-free, *gracias*.'

She laughed. 'Picky, picky! Most men wouldn't mind.'

Perfect teeth gleamed in the semi-darkness of the limo. 'I am not most men. No doubt you'll add *that* to my list of flaws?'

His eyes dropped to her chest, abruptly cutting off her laughter.

'You had better not be examining me for silicone. I'll have you know these babies are natural.'

'Trust me, I can tell the difference,' he said, in a low, intense voice.

She swallowed hard. The thought that she was suddenly treading unsafe waters descended on her. Frantically, she cast her mind around for a safe subject.

'So you don't like clubbing?'

'It's not how I choose to spend an evening, no.'

'Let me guess—you're the starchy opera type?'

'Wrong again.'

She snapped her fingers. 'I know—you like to stay indoors and watch game shows.'

Low laughter greeted her announcement. Deep inside, a tiny part of Sasha performed a freakishly disturbing happy dance.

Encouraged, she pressed on. 'Telemetry reports and aerodynamic calculations?'

'Now you're getting warm.'

'Ha! I knew you were a closet nerd!'

He cast her a wry glance. 'I prefer to call it passion.'

She shrugged. 'A passionate nerd who surrounds himself with a crowd but keeps his distance.'

He stiffened. 'You're psychoanalysing me again.'

'You make it easy.'

'And *you* make baseless assumptions.'

'Good try, but you can't freeze me out with that tone. You're single-minded to the point of obsession. I wiki-ed you. You have more money than you could ever spend in ten lifetimes and yet you don't let anyone close. You have the odd liaison, but nothing that lasts more than a few weeks. According to your girlfriends, you never stay over. And there's a time limit on every relationship.'

'You shouldn't believe everything you read—especially in the tabloid press.'

'Tell me which part is false,' she challenged.

His gaze hardened. 'I'll tell you which part is right—every relationship ends. For ever is a concept made up to sell romance novels.'

'Didn't you have a long liaison once, when you were still racing? What was her name…? Angela? Ange—?'

'Angelique,' he bit out, his face frozen as if hewn from rock. 'And she wasn't a liaison. We were engaged.'

'She must be the reason, then.'

Cold eyes slammed into her. 'The reason?'

'For the way you are?'

'Did Derek Mahoney turn you into the intrusive woman you are today?' he fired back, his tone rougher than sandpaper. 'Because I'd like to find him and throttle the life out of him.'

Sasha knew she should let it go. But somehow she couldn't.

'Yes. No.' She sighed and looked out of the window at Kensington's nightlife. 'Damn, I wish I smoked.'

An astounded breath whistled from his lips. 'Why would you wish that?'

'Because trying to have a conversation with you is exhausting enough to drive anyone to drink. But since I have to be up at the crack of dawn tomorrow, and I've reached my one-glass drink limit, smoking would be the other choice—if I smoked.' Abandoning the view, she turned back to him. 'Where was I?'

A mirthless smile lifted one corner of his mouth. 'You were dissecting my life and finding it severely deficient.'

'Mockery? Is that your default setting?'

He lowered his gaze to her lips and her insides clenched so hard she feared she'd break in half. The limo turned a sharp corner. She grabbed the armrest to steady herself. Too late she realised the action had thrust her breasts out. Marco's gaze dropped lower. Heat pooled in her belly. Her breasts ached, feeling fuller than they'd ever felt.

He leaned closer. Her heart thundered.

'No, Sasha,' he said hoarsely. '*This* is my default setting.'

Strong hands cupped her cheeks, held her steady. Heat-filled eyes stared into hers, their shocking intensity igniting a fire deep inside her.

Sasha held her breath, almost afraid to move in case…in case…

He fastened his mouth to hers, tumbling her into a none-too-gentle kiss that sent the blood racing through her veins. He tasted of heat and wine, of tensile strength and fiery Latin willpower. Of red-blooded passion and intoxicating pleasure. And he went straight to her head.

Sasha felt a groan rise in her throat and abruptly shut it off. She wasn't *that* easy. Although right now, with Marco's mouth wreaking insane havoc on her blood pressure, *easy* was deliciously tempting.

His tongue caressed hers and the groan slipped through, echoing in the dim cavern of the moving car. One hand slipped to her nape, angling her head. Although he didn't need to. She was willingly tilting her head, all the better to deepen the pressure and pleasure of his kiss. Her mouth opened, boldly inviting him in.

His moan made her triumphant and weak at the same time. Then she lost all thought but of the bliss of the kiss.

Lost all sense of time.

Until she heard the thud of a door.

Their lips parted with a loud, sucking noise that arrowed straight to the furnace-hot apex of her thighs.

Marco stared down at her, his breath shaking out of his chest. *'Dios,'* he muttered after several tense, disbelieving seconds.

You can say that again. Thankfully, the words didn't materialise on her lips. Her eyes fell to his mouth, still wet from their kiss, and the heat between her legs increased a thousandfold.

Get a grip, Sasha. She reined herself in and pulled away as reality sank in. She'd kissed Marco de Cervantes—fallen into him like a drowning swimmer fell on a life raft.

'We're here,' he rasped, setting her free abruptly to spear a hand through his hair.

'Y-yes,' she mumbled, cringing when her voice emerged low and desire-soaked.

With one last look at her, he thrust his door open and helped her out.

They entered the exclusive apartment complex in silence, travelled up to the penthouse suite in silence. Sasha made sure she placed herself as far from him as possible.

After shutting the apartment door he turned to her. Sasha held her breath, guilt rising to mix with the desire that still churned so frantically through her.

'I have an early start—'

'Sasha—'

Marco gestured for her to go first.

Sasha cleared her throat, keeping her gaze on his chest so he wouldn't see the conflicting emotions in her eyes. 'I have an early start tomorrow. So…um…goodnight.'

After a long, heavy pause, he nodded. 'I think that's a good idea. *Buenos noches.'*

All the way down the plushly carpeted hallway she felt his

gaze on her. Even after she shut the door behind her his presence lingered.

Dropping her clutch bag, she traced her fingers over her lips. They still tingled, along with every inch of her body. Resting her head against the door, she sucked in a desperate breath.

One hand drifted over her midriff to her pelvis, where desire gripped her in an unbearable vice of need. A need she had every intention of denying, no matter how strong.

Wanting Marco de Cervantes was a mistake. Even if there was the remotest possibility of a relationship between them it would be over in a matter of weeks. And she knew without a shadow of a doubt that it would also spell the end of her career.

And her experience with Derek had taught that no man— no matter how intensely charismatic, no matter how great a kisser— was worth the price of her dreams.

CHAPTER SEVEN

'COFFEE…I smell coffee,' she mumbled into the pillow, the murky fog of her brain teasing her with the seductive aroma of caffeine. 'Please, God, let there be coffee when I open my eyes.'

Carefully she cracked one eye open. Marco stood at the foot of her bed, in a dark green T-shirt and jeans, a steaming mug in his hand.

'If I demand to know what you're doing in my bedroom so early, will you withhold that coffee from me?'

There was no smile this morning, just an even, cool stare, but awareness drummed beneath the surface of her skin nonetheless.

'It's not early. It's eight o'clock.'

With a groan, she levered herself up, braced her back against the headboard. 'Eight o'clock is the crack of dawn, Marco.' She held out her hand for the cup. He didn't move. 'Please,' she croaked.

With an uncharacteristically jerky movement he rounded the bed and handed it to her. Sasha tried not to let her eyes linger on the taut inch of golden-tanned skin that was revealed when he stretched. Her brain couldn't handle anything so overwhelming. Not just yet.

She took her first sip, groaned with pleasure and sagged against the pillow.

'You're not a morning person, are you?'

'Oops, my secret is out. I think whoever decreed that anything was important enough to start before ten o'clock in the morning should be hung, drawn and quartered.' She cradled the warm mug in her hand. 'Okay, I guess now I'm awake enough to ask what you're doing in my room.'

'I knocked. Several times.'

She grimaced. 'I sleep like the dead sometimes.' She took another grateful sip and just stopped herself from moaning again. Moans were bad. 'How did you know to bring me coffee?'

'I know everything about you,' he answered.

Her heart lurched, but she managed to keep her face straight. Marco didn't know about her baby. And she meant to keep it that way.

'I forgot. You have mad voodoo skills.'

His eyes strayed up from where he'd been examining the vampire on her T-shirt. 'No voodoo. Just mad skills. As to why I'm here—I have a meeting in the city in forty-five minutes—'

'On a Saturday?' She caught his wry glance. 'Oh, never mind.'

'I wanted to discuss last night before I left.'

Her breath stalled in her chest. 'Yes. Last night. We kissed.'

A sharp hiss issued from his lips. Then, '*Sí*, we did.'

She bravely met his gaze, even as her heart hammered. 'Before you condemn me for it, you need to know I don't make a habit of that sort of thing.'

His very Latin shrug drew her eyes to the bold, strong outline of his shoulders. 'And yet it happened.'

'We could blame the wine? Oh, wait, you barely touched your glass all evening.'

'How would you know? You were neck-deep in discussing the Premier League.'

She sighed. 'What can I say? I love my footie. Which club do you support?'

'Barcelona.'

She grimaced. 'Of course. You seem the Barcelona type.'

He shook his head. 'I don't even want to know what that means.'

Silence encased them. She took a few more sips of her coffee, instinctively sensing she'd need the caffeine boost to withstand what was coming.

Marco raised his head and looked at her. The tormented gleam in his eyes stopped her breath. 'What happened last night will not happen again.'

Despite telling herself the very same thing over and over last night, she felt a sharp dart of disappointment and hurt lance through her. She feigned a casual tone. 'I agree.'

'You belong to my brother,' he carried on, as if she hadn't spoken.

'I belong to no one. I'm my own person.'

His gaze speared hers. 'It can't happen again.'

Again the uncomfortable dart of pain. 'And I agreed with you. Are you trying to convince me or yourself?'

He shook his head. 'You know, I've never met anyone so forthright.'

'I believe in being upfront. I'm nobody's yes-woman. You need to know that right now. I kiss whomever I want. But kissing you was a mistake. One that I hope will not jeopardise my contract.'

His gaze hardened. 'You value being a racing driver more than personal relationships?'

'I haven't had a successful run with relationships but I'm a brilliant driver. I think it's wise to stick to doing what I do best. And I'd prefer not to lose my job because you feel guilty over a simple kiss. I also understand if you have some reservations because of your brother. Really, it's no big deal. There's no need to beat yourself up over it.'

Running out of oxygen, she clamped her mouth shut.

This was yet another reason why she hated mornings. At this time of day the natural barrier between her brain and her mouth was severely weakened.

Throw in the fruitless soul-searching she'd done into the wee hours, and the resultant sleep-deprivation, and who knew what would come of out her mouth next?

He shoved a forceful hand through his hair. '*Dios*, this has nothing to do with your contract. If you were mine to take I'd have no reservations. None. The things I would do to you. *With* you.'

He named a few.

Her mouth dropped open.

Lust singed the air, its fumes thick and heavy. Her fingers clenched around her mug. Silently, desperately, she willed it away. But her body wasn't prepared to heed her. Underneath her T-shirt her nipples reacted to his words, tightening into painful, needy buds.

'Wow! That's...um...super, *super*-naughty.'

Hazel eyes snapped pure fire at her. 'And that's just for starters,' he rasped.

Her breath strangled in her chest.

In another life, at another time...

No! Even in a parallel universe having anything to do with Marco would be bad news.

'I hear a *but* somewhere in there. Either you still think I'm poison or it's something else. Tell me. I can take it.'

He gave a jerky nod of his head in a move she was becoming familiar with. 'Last night, at the awards, you spoke of Rafael like a friend.'

'Because that's what he is. Just a friend.'

His jaw clenched. 'You're asking me to take your word over my brother's?'

'Not really. I'm saying give us both the benefit of the doubt. See where it takes you.'

He shook his head. 'As long as Rafael sees you as his there can be nothing between us.'

Despite the steaming coffee in her hand, she felt a chill spread through her. 'The message has been received, loud and clear. Was there something else?'

For a full minute he didn't answer. Then, 'I don't want you to think that the kiss has bought you any special privileges.'

'You mean like expecting you to bring me coffee every morning?' she replied sarcastically, a surprisingly acute pain scouring its acidic path through her belly.

'My expectations from you as a driver haven't changed. In fact nothing has changed. Understood?'

Setting down her mug on the bedside table, she hugged her

knees. 'All this angst over a simple kiss, Marco?' The need to reduce the kiss to an inconsequential blip burned through her, despite her body's insistence on reliving it.

He prowled to the window and turned to face her. 'Women have a habit of reading more into a situation than there actually is.' His raised hand killed her response. 'While taking pains to state the contrary. But I want to be very clear—I don't *do* relationships.'

Her breath fractured in her lungs. 'I'm not looking for one,' she forced out.

His whole body stiffened. 'Then it stands to reason that there shouldn't be a problem.'

She hugged her knees tighter. 'Again I sense a *but*.'

'*But*…for some reason you're all I think about.'

The statement was delivered with joyless candour. Yet her heart leapt like a puppet whose string had been jerked. And when his eyes met hers and she saw the heat in them something inside her melted.

He strode back towards the bed, shoving clenched fists into his pockets. She stared up at him, her pulse racing. 'And you're annoyed about that?'

His gaze raked her face slowly. Then slid to her neck, her breasts, and back up again. Molten heat burned in his eyes. 'Livid. Frustrated. Puzzled. Intensely aroused.'

Of their own volition her eyes dropped below his belt-line. Confronted with the evidence, she felt a deep longing melt between her legs. She swallowed as heat poured through her whole being.

Looking away, she muttered, 'Don't do that.'

A strained sound escaped his throat. 'I was just about to demand the same of you.'

'I'm not doing anything. You, on the other hand—you're…' She sucked in a desperate breath.

'I'm what?' he demanded, his voice low, ferocious.

'You're all brooding and…and fierce…and angry…and… aroused. You're cursing your desire for me and yet your eyes are promising all sorts of rampant steaminess.' Her eyes darted back to the bulge in his trousers and a lump clogged her throat. 'I…I think you should leave.'

'You don't sound very sure about that.'

'*I am.* I don't want you. And even if I did you're off-limits to me, remember? So you can't…can't present me with…*this*!'

A pulse jerked in his jaw. 'I never said the situation wasn't without complications.'

'Well, the solution is easy. You hired me to do a job so let me get on with it. We don't have to see each other until the season ends and we win the Constructors' Championship. We'll stand on the top podium and douse ourselves in champagne. Then we'll go our separate ways until next season starts.'

'And you will have fulfilled this promise you made?'

Surprise zapped through her. He remembered. 'Partly, yes,' she replied, before thinking better of it.

His gaze turned speculative. 'To whom did you make the promise?'

She dragged her eyes from his, the sudden need to spill everything shocking her with its intensity. But she couldn't. Marco didn't trust her. And she wasn't prepared to trust him with the sacred memory of her father.

She shook her head. 'It's none of your business. Are you going to leave me alone to get on with it?'

His mouth firmed into a hard line. 'The team has too much riding on this for me to take my eye off the ball at this juncture. So do our sponsors. Once you have proved yourself—'

'Yes, I've heard it all before.' She couldn't stop the bitterness from spilling out. 'Prove myself. Don't bewitch anyone on the team. *Especially* not the boss. Message received and understood. Perhaps you could take your frustrations elsewhere, then, and spare me the thwarted lust backlash?'

He stiffened with anger. '*Dios.* Has no one ever told you that the difference between attractive feistiness and maddening shrew is one bitchy comment too many?'

'No one has dared,' she threw back.

'Well, take it from me. You need to stop throwing blind punches and learn to pick your fights.' He strode towards the door. 'Romano will drive you to your appointment and bring you back here.'

'That's not necessary. I've hired a scooter.'

He whirled to face her. 'No. Romano will drive you.' His tone brooked no argument.

'Seriously, Marco, you need to dial back the caveman stuff—'

'And *you* need to take greater responsibility for your welfare. If you come off your scooter and break an arm or a leg the rest of the season is finished. I thought you wanted the drive? Or do you think you're invincible on those little piles of junk you like to travel on?'

She bit back a heated retort. Marco was right. All her hard work and sacrifice would amount to nothing if she couldn't ensure she turned up to her races with her bones intact.

'Fine. I'll use the car.'

Pushing back the covers, she slid her feet over the edge and stood. The air thickened once more as Marco tensed.

Sasha refused to look into his face. His brooding, tempting heat would weaken her sorely tested resolve.

'I need to get ready for the shoot.'

He made a sound she couldn't decipher. She squeezed her thighs together and fingered the hem of her T-shirt.

'Your breakfast will be delivered in half an hour.' He moved towards the door. 'Oh, and Sasha…?'

Unable to stop herself, she looked. Framed in the doorway, his stature was impressively male and utterly arresting. 'Yes?' she rasped.

'Unless you want things to slide out of control, don't wear that T-shirt in my presence again. You may not be mine, but I'm not a saint. The next time I see you in it I may feel obliged to take advantage of its instruction.'

His words hit her with the force of a tsunami. By the time he shut the door, a hundred different images of Marco using his teeth on her had short-circuited her brain.

The photo shoot was horrendously tedious. Several hours of sitting around getting her hair and make-up done, followed by a frenzied half-hour of striking impossible poses, then back to repeating the whole process again.

Sasha returned to the hotel very near exhaustion, but she had gained a healthy respect for models. She also now understood why men like Marco dated them. The sample pictures the photographer had let her keep showed an end result that surprised her.

After pressing the button for the lift, she fished the pictures out of her satchel, shocked all over again by how different she looked—how a few strokes of a make-up brush could transform plain to almost...*sexy*. Or was it something else? All day she'd been unable to dismiss last night's kiss from her mind. Her face burned when she reached the picture of her licking her tingling lips. She'd been recalling Marco's moan of pleasure as he'd deepened their kiss.

So really it was Marco's fault...

Opening the door to the suite, she stopped in her tracks as strains of jazz music wafted in from the living room. Following the sound, she entered the large, opulent room to find Marco lounging on the sofa, an electronic tablet in his hand and a glass of red wine on a table beside him.

'I thought you were going to be late?' The words rushed out before she could stop them. Her suddenly racing pulse made her dizzy for a few seconds.

His gaze zeroed in on her. 'I wrapped things up early.'

'And you couldn't find anyone in your little black book to spend the evening with?'

The thought that he hadn't gone out and vented his sexual frustration on some entirely willing female sent a bolt of elation through her, which she tried—unsuccessfully—to smash down.

She couldn't read the hooded look in his eyes as he set aside the gadget.

'It's only seven-thirty. The night is still young,' he replied.

Something crumpled into a small, tight knot inside her, and the sharp pang she'd felt that morning returned. 'That's just typical. You're going to call some poor woman out of the blue and expect her to be ready to drop everything to go out with you, aren't you?' she mocked.

One corner of his mouth quirked. 'Luckily, the women I know are kind enough to *want* to drop everything for me.'

She snorted. 'Come off it. We both know kindness has nothing to do with it.'

As she'd seen first-hand at the awards ceremony, women would crawl over hot coals to be with Marco. And many more would do so regardless of his financial status or influence. With a body and face like his, he could be penniless and still attract women with a snap of his fingers. As for that lethal, rarely seen smile, and the way he kissed—

Her thoughts screeched to a halt as he stood and came towards her.

'Maybe not,' he conceded, with not a hint of arrogance in sight. 'How was the shoot?'

The question wrenched her from her avid scrutiny of his body. 'Aside from the free shoes, it was a pain in the ass,' she replied.

'Of course,' he agreed gravely. Then without warning he reached out and plucked the pictures from her fingers. 'Maybe you'll even get around to wearing them instead of going barefoot or wearing those hideous boots—'

He stopped speaking as he stared at the pictures. Awareness crawled across her skin as he slowly thumbed through them, lingering over the one where she was draped over the bonnet of the not-yet-released prototype of his latest car, the Cervantes Triunfo. Eventually he returned to *that* one. And looked as if he'd stopped breathing.

'Marco…'

She stretched out her hand to retrieve the pictures. He ignored her, his attention fixed on the picture, his skin drawn tight over the chiselled bones of his face.

'Marco, I don't want to keep you. I have plans of my own.'

His head snapped up. 'What plans?' he demanded, his tone rough and tight.

Sasha couldn't think how to answer. Her whole mind was

paralysed by the way his eyes blazed. Shaking her head, she tried to turn away. He grabbed her arm in a firm hold.

No! Too hot. Too irresistible. Too much.

'Let me go,' she murmured, her voice scraped raw with desire.

'What plans?' he gritted out.

'Are you sure you want to know? You may not approve.'

His hand tightened on her arm, his eyes darkening into storm clouds that threatened thunder and lightning. 'Then think carefully before you speak.'

She sighed. 'Fine. You've busted me. I was going to beg your chef to make me that T-bone steak and salad he made for us yesterday, followed by chocolate caramel delight for dessert— I'll think about the calories later. Afterwards I intend to have a sweltering foursome with Joel, LuAnn and Logan.'

The hand that had started to relax suddenly tightened, harder than before.

'Excuse me?' Marco bit out, his voice a thin blade of ice slicing across her skin.

Reaching into the handbag slung over her shoulder, she pulled out the boxed set of her favourite TV vampire show.

He released her and reached for it. After scrutinising it, he threw it down onto the sofa along with the pictures.

'Take a piece of advice for free, *pequeña*. It's a mistake to keep goading me. The consequences will be greater than you ever bargained for.' His voice was soft. Deadly soft.

Sasha felt a shiver go through her. Most people mistakenly assumed partaking in one of the most dangerous sports in the world meant X1 Premier Racing drivers were fearless. Sasha wasn't fearless. She had a healthy amount of fear and respect for her profession. She knew when to accelerate, when to pull back the throttle, when to pull over and abandon her car.

Right now the look on Marco's face warned her she was skidding close to danger. She heeded the warning. Lashing out because of the maelstrom of emotions roiling inside her would most likely result in far worse consequences than she'd endured with Derek.

'Understood. Let me go.'

Surprise at her easy capitulation lit his eyes. Abruptly he released her.

'I need a shower. I guess you'll be gone when I come out. Enjoy your evening.'

Shamelessly, she fled.

Marco watched her go, frustration and bewilderment fighting a messy battle inside him.

He prided himself on knowing and understanding women. After Angelique, his determination never to be caught out again had decreed it. Women liked to think they were complicated creatures, but when it came down to it their needs were basic, no matter how much they tried to hide it. Hell, some—like Angelique—even spelled it out.

'I want fame, Marco. I want excitement! I can't be with a man who's a has-been.'

The memory slid in, reminding him why he now ensured the women he associated with knew there was no rosy future in store for them and had no surprises waiting to trap him.

A reality devoid of surprises suited him just fine.

His eyes followed Sasha's tall, slim figure down the hallway.

She surprised him, he admitted reluctantly. She also infuriated him. She made his blood boil in a way that was so basic, so...*sexual*—even without the benefit of those pictures...

Dios! With a growl, he whirled towards the window. When he'd gone to her room to set things straight this morning the last thing he'd expected was for her to reassure him that it had been no big deal.

Despite being totally into the kiss—as much as he'd been—she'd walked away from him last night. A situation he'd never encountered before.

Was it because she didn't really want him? Or was she merely waiting for his brother to wake up so she could resume where they'd left off?

Acid burned through his stomach at the thought. But even the corrosive effect couldn't wash away the underlying sexual need that seared him.

He'd rushed through his meeting with every intention of calling one of the many willing female acquaintances on his BlackBerry. But once he'd returned, his need to go out again had waned. He withdrew from examining why too closely.

He turned back from the window and his eyes fell on the pictures on the sofa. To the one of her draped all over his car...

Blindly he stumbled towards his jacket and dug around for his phone. Two minutes later reservations were made. By the time his Rolls collected him from the foyer, Sasha Fleming had been consigned to the furthest corner of his mind.

Marco stood outside the door ninety minutes later, caught himself listening for sounds from inside, and grimaced in disbelief. He'd spent the last hour or so wining and dining a woman whose name he couldn't now remember.

He'd stared at his date's in-your-face scarlet lips and thought of another set of lips. Plump, freshly licked lips, captured in perfect celluloid. Lips that had responded to his kiss in a way that had sent the most potent pulse of excitement through him.

Forbidden lips.

In the end he'd thrown down his napkin and extracted several large notes. 'You'll have to forgive me. I'm terrible company to-night. I shouldn't have disturbed your evening.'

The practised pout had reappeared. 'You know I'll forgive you anything, Marco.'

Candy? Candice? had leaned forward in another carefully calculated pose, designed to showcase her body to its best advantage.

'Listen, I have an idea. I know how much you like your coffee. When I was filming in Brazil last month I absolutely fell in love with the coffee and brought some back with me. Why don't we skip dessert and go back to my place and I'll give you a taste?'

Barely containing rising distaste, he'd shaken his head. 'Sorry, I'll take a rain check.'

He'd led her out amid soft protests and further throaty promises of the delights of her cafetière. But coffee, or sex with Candy/Candice had been the last thing on his mind.

His sudden hunger for chocolate caramel had become over-powering.

'Take my car. I'll walk,' he'd said.

And now here he stood, skulking outside his own apartment like a hormonal teenager on his first date.

He entered and approached the living room.

She was curled up on the sofa, a bowl of popcorn in her lap. Her head snapped towards him. As if she'd been listening out for him too. The thought pleased him more than it should have.

The striking blue of her eyes paralysed him.

'You're still awake.' *Excelente, Marco. First prize for stating the obvious.*

She blinked. 'It's only nine-fifteen.' Her eyes followed him as he shrugged off his jacket and dropped it on the sofa. When her gaze lingered on his chest he felt the blood surge stronger than before.

He watched her fingers dance through the bowl of popcorn, the movement curiously erotic. His heart hammered harder. 'You didn't have the chocolate caramel after all?'

'Charlie's disapproving face haunted me. Popcorn is healthier.' She looked away. 'So, how was your date?' she asked, her voice husky.

He wrenched his gaze from her fingers. 'You really want to know?'

Her sensual lips firmed and she shook her head.

The need to gauge her true feelings drew him closer. 'Jealous?'

She inhaled sharply. 'I thought we weren't doing this?'

His eyes fell to her lips. 'Maybe I've changed my mind.'

'Well, change it back. Nothing has changed since this morning. I can't handle your…baggage. And I don't want a relationship. Of any sort.'

Marco opened his mouth to tell her he didn't want anything from her either. But he knew he was lying. His very presence in this room belied that.

Forbidden or not, he wanted her with a compulsive need that unnerved and baffled him. But the fact that he wanted her didn't mean he would have her. He was known for his legendary control. He sat down next to her, caught her scent, and simply willed himself not to react.

Forcing his body to relax, he nodded towards the television. 'You have a thing for vampires?'

'Doesn't everyone?' she replied breathlessly.

He wanted to look at her. But he denied himself the urge and kept his gaze fixed ahead. 'What's the story about?'

She hesitated, fidgeted and sat forward. From the corner of his eye he saw her lick her lips. Fiery heat sang through his veins.

'Oh, you know—it's the usual run-of-the-mill storyline. Two brothers in love with the same girl.'

Something tightened in his chest and his stomach muscles clenched. 'I see.'

'You don't have to watch it.' She shifted backwards, out of his periphery.

'Why not? I'm intrigued.' The two male protagonists faced off on the screen, fangs bared. 'What are they doing now?'

Again she hesitated. 'They're about to fight to the death for her.'

His muscles pulled tighter. Blood surged through his veins and he forcibly relaxed the clenched fist on his thigh.

'Which one are you rooting for?' he asked, the skin on his nape curiously tight as he waited for her answer.

It occurred to him how absurd the conversation was. How absurd it was to be so wound up by a TV show. But every second he waited for her answer felt like an eternity.

'Neither.'

Illogically, his insides hollowed. 'You don't care if either one of them dies?' The words grated his throat.

'That's not what I said. I said neither because I know they won't kill each other. They might tear chunks out of each other, but ultimately they love each other too much to let a woman come between them. No matter how difficult, or how heart-wrenching it is to watch, I know they'll work it out. That's why I love the show. Popcorn?'

The bowl appeared in front of him.

He declined and nodded at the screen as a female character walked on. 'Is she the one?'

Sasha laughed. 'Yep. LuAnn—*femme fatale extraordinaire*. With those huge brown eyes and that body she can have any man she wants. On *and* off the screen.'

'She may look innocent onscreen but off-screen is another matter.'

It was her gasp that did it. That and her scent, mingled with the strangely enticing aroma of popcorn.

Control failed and his eyes met Sasha's stunning blue. Marco wondered if she knew how enthralling they were. How captivating. How very easily she could give LuAnn a run for her money.

'You've met her?'

'Briefly. At one of Rafael's parties.'

Her eyes returned to the screen. 'As much as I'm dying to know the details of your no-doubt salacious meeting, I don't really want the illusion spoiled. Do you mind?'

Again Marco was struck by Sasha's contrast to the other women he'd dated. They would have been bowled over by his mention of a celebrity, dying to know every single detail. Her refreshingly indifferent attitude made him relax a little more.

When he found himself munching on popcorn another bolt of surprise shot through him.

When was the last time he'd relaxed completely like this? Shared an enjoyable evening with a woman that hadn't ended in sex if he'd wanted it to?

He glanced at Sasha. Her eyes were glued to the screen, her lower lip caught between her teeth. Heat ratcheted through him. Correction—an evening that wasn't going to end in sex because sex was forbidden?

He reached for another mouthful of popcorn and his hand brushed hers. Her breath caught but she didn't look away from the screen. When he reluctantly forced his gaze away from her, he saw LuAnn caught in a heated clinch with Joel.

As a thirty-five-year-old man, who knew that sex onscreen was simulated, he shouldn't have found the scene erotic. Especially not with those damned fangs thrown in.

Nevertheless, when Sasha's breath caught for a second time he turned to her, his heart pounding so loudly in his ears he couldn't hear anything else.

'You should be watching the screen, not me.'

Her husky murmur thrummed along his nerve-endings and made a beeline for his groin.

'I was never much of a spectator. I prefer to be a participant.'

Dios! He was hard—so hard it was a toss-up as to whether the feeling was pain or pleasure. The logical thing to do was to get up, walk away.

Yet he couldn't move. Couldn't look away from this woman his body ached for but his mind knew he couldn't have.

Her eyes found his. 'Marco...'

Again it was a husky entreaty.

His fingers brushed her cheek. 'Why can't I get you out of my head? I took a beautiful woman to dinner but I can barely remember what she looked like now. I ate but hardly tasted the food. All I could think about was you.'

'Do you want me to apologise?'

'Would you mean it?'

Her pink tongue darted out, licked, darted back in. He groaned in pain.

'Probably not. But I may have an explanation for you.'

A few feet away the TV belted out the closing sequence of the show. Neither of them paid any attention. His forefinger traced her soft skin to the corner of her mouth, the need to taste her again a raging fever flaming through his veins. 'I'm listening.'

She shrugged. 'Maybe you share a trait with your brother after all. Deny you something and you want it more?'

Marco didn't need to think about it to answer. 'No. The difference between Rafael and me is that he wouldn't have hesitated to take—consequences be damned. He sees something he wants and he takes it.'

'Whereas you agonise about it endlessly, then deny yourself anyway? It's almost as if you're testing yourself—putting yourself through some sort of punishment.'

Her eyes darkened when he froze. She moved her head and

her lips came closer to his finger. Marco couldn't speak, needing every single ounce of self-control to keep his shock from showing. He *deserved* to put himself through punishment for what he'd done. He'd lost the most precious thing in life—a child—because he'd taken his eye off the ball.

'Maybe you should learn to bend a little…take what is being offered? What is being offered freely.'

An arrow of pain shot through the haze of desire engulfing him. He gave a single shake of his head and inhaled. 'I stopped believing in *free* a long time ago, Sasha. There are always consequences. The piper always expects payment.'

'I don't believe that. Laughter is free. Love is free. It's hate that eats you up inside. Bitterness that twists feelings if you let them. And, no, I'm not waxing philosophical. I've experienced it.'

'Really?' he mocked, dropping his hand. When his senses screeched in protest he merely willed the feeling away. 'To whom did you make your promise?' he asked, the need to know as forceful as the need raging through his veins.

Wariness darkened her eyes. Then her shoulders rolled. 'My father.'

'What did you promise him?'

'That I'd win the Drivers' Championship for him.'

'Out of some misguided sense of duty, no doubt?' he derided.

Anger blazed through her eyes. 'Not duty. *Love.* And it's about as misguided as your bullheaded need to coddle Rafael.'

'There's a difference between responsibility and your illusionary love,' he rebutted, irate at this turn of the conversation.

'I suffer no illusions. My father loved me as unconditionally as I loved him.'

Tensing, he sat back in the seat. 'Then you were lucky. Not everyone is imbued with unconditional love for his or her child. Some even use their unborn children as bartering tools.'

Her breath caught. 'Did you…? Are you saying that from experience?'

A cold drench of reality washed over him at how close he'd come to revealing everything.

Surging to his feet, he stared into her face. 'I was merely making a point. As much as I want you, Sasha, I'll never take you. The consequences would be too great.'

CHAPTER EIGHT

THE consequences would be too great.

Sasha tried to block out the words as she adjusted the traction control on her steering wheel. The tremor in her fingers increased and she clenched her fists tighter around the wheel.

Shears, Marina Bay, Raffles Boulevard. Watch out for Turn Ten speed bump—Padang, pit lane exit, look after the tyres...

Her heart hammered, excitement and adrenaline shooting through her as she went through the rigorous ritual of visualising every corner of the race. At her third attempt, fear rose to mingle with her emotions.

She'd secured pole position for the first time in her racing career, but despite the team's euphoria afterwards she'd sensed a subtle waning of their excitement as speculation as to whether she could do the job trickled in. Sasha had seen it in their faces, heard it in Luke's voice this morning when he'd grilled her over race strategy for the millionth time. Even Tom had weighed in.

Consequences...responsibility...last chance...

Sweat trickled down her neck and she hastily sipped at her water tube. She couldn't afford dehydration. Couldn't afford to lose focus. In fact she couldn't afford to do anything less than win.

Beyond the bright lights of the circuit that turned night into day at the Singapore Grand Prix thousands of fans would be watching.

As would Marco.

He hadn't spoken to her since that night on his sofa in London, but he'd attended every race since the season had resumed and Sasha knew he was somewhere above her, in the exclusive VIP suite of the team's motor home, hosting the Prime Minister, royalty and a never-ending stream of celebrities.

Some time during the sleepless night, when she'd been looking down at the race track from her hotel room, she'd wondered whether he'd even bother to grace the pit with his presence if she made it onto that final elusive step on the podium. Or whether he would be too preoccupied with entertaining his latest flame—the blonde daughter of an Italian textile magnate who never seemed far from his side nowadays.

She tried desperately to block him from her mind. Taking pole position today—a dream she'd held for longer than she could remember—should be making her ecstatic. She was one step further towards removing the dark stain of her father's shame from people's minds. To finally removing herself from Derek's malingering shadow.

Yet all she could think about was Marco and their conversation in London.

She clenched her teeth in frustration and breathed in deeply.

Luke's voice piped through her helmet, disrupting her thoughts.

'Adjust your clutch—'

She flicked the switch before he'd finished speaking. The sheer force of her will to win was a force field around her. Finally she found the zen she desperately craved.

Focusing, she followed the red lights as they lit up one by one. Adrenaline rushed faster, followed a second later by the drag of the powerful car as she pointed it towards the first corner.

She made it by the skin of her teeth, narrowly missing the front wing of the number two driver. Her stomach churned through lap after gruelling lap, even after she'd established a healthy distance between her and the car behind.

What seemed like an eternity later, after a frenzied race, including an unscheduled pitstop that had raised the hairs on her arms, she heard the frenzied shouts of her race engineer in her ear.

'You won! Sasha, you won the Singapore Grand Prix!'

Tears prickled her eyes even as her fist pumped through the air. Her father's face floated through her mind and a sense of peace settled momentarily over her. It was broken a second later by the sound of the crowd's deafening roar.

Exiting the car, Sasha squinted through the bright flashes of the paparazzi, desperate to see familiar hazel eyes through the sea of faces screaming her name.

No Marco.

A stab of disappointment hollowed out her stomach. With a sense of detachment, she accepted the congratulations of her fellow drivers and blinked back tears through the British national anthem.

Dad would be proud, she reminded herself fiercely. *He* was all that mattered. Plastering a smile on her face, she accepted her trophy from the Prime Minister.

This was what she wanted. What she'd fought for. The team— *her* team—were cheering wildly. Yet Sasha felt numb inside.

Fighting the alarming emptiness, she picked up the obligatory champagne magnum, letting the spray loose over her fellow podium winners. Brusquely she told herself to live in the moment, to enjoy the dream-come-true experience of winning her first race.

Camera flashes blinded her as she stepped off the podium. When it cleared Tom stood in front of her, a huge grin on his face.

'I *knew* you could do it! Prepare yourself, Sasha. Your world's about to rock!'

The obligatory press conference for the top three winning drivers took half an hour. When she emerged, Tom grabbed her arm and steered her towards the bank of reporters waiting behind the barriers.

'Tom, I don't really want—'

'You've just won your first race. *"I don't really want"* shouldn't feature in your vocabulary. The world's your oyster.'

But I don't want the world, she screamed silently. *I want Marco. I want not to feel alone on a night like this.*

Feeling the stupid tears build again, Sasha rapidly blinked them back as a microphone was thrust in her face.

'How does it feel to be the first woman to win the Singapore Grand Prix?'

From deep inside she summoned a smile. 'Just as brilliant as the first man felt when he won, I expect.'

Beside her she heard Tom's sharp intake of breath.

Behave, Sasha.

'Are you still involved with Rafael de Cervantes?' asked an odious reporter she recognised from a Brazilian sports channel.

'Rafael and I were never involved. We're just friends.'

'So now he's in a coma there's nothing to stop you from switching *friendships* to his brother, no?'

Tom stepped forward. 'Listen, mate—'

Sasha stopped him. 'No. It's fine.' She faced the reporter. 'Marco de Cervantes is a world-class engineer and a visionary in his field. His incredible race car design is the reason we won the race today. It would be an honour for me to call him my friend.' She tagged on another smile and watched the reporter's face droop with disappointment.

Tom nodded at a British female reporter. 'Next question.'

'As the winner of the race, you'll be the guest of honour at the rock concert. What will you be wearing?'

Mild shock went through her at the question, followed swiftly by a deepening sense of hollowness. The X1 Premier Rock Concert had become a fixture on every A-List celebrity's calendar. No doubt Marco would be there with his latest girlfriend.

'It doesn't matter what I'll be wearing because I'm not going to the concert.'

Sasha dashed into the foyer of her six-star hotel, grateful when the two burly doormen blocked the chasing paparazzi. She heaved in a sigh of relief when she shut her suite door behind her.

The ever-widening chasm of emptiness she couldn't shake threatened to overwhelm her. Quickly she stripped off her clothes and showered.

The knock came as she was towelling herself dry. For a second she considered not answering it.

A sense of *déjà vu* hit her as she opened the door to another perfectly coiffed stylist, carting another rack of clothes.

'I think you've got the wrong suite.'

The diminutive Asian woman in a pink suit simply bowed, smiled and let herself in. Her assistant sailed in behind her, clutching a large and stunningly beautiful bouquet of purple lilies and cream roses.

'For you.' She thrust the flowers and a long oblong box into Sasha's hand.

Stifling a need to scream, Sasha calmly shut the door and opened the box. On a red velvet cushion lay the most exquisite diamond necklace she'd ever seen. With shaking fingers, she plucked the card from the tiny peg.

Pick a dress, then they'll leave. Romano is waiting downstairs.

Sasha stared at Marco's bold scrawl in disbelief. When she looked up, the women smiled and started pulling clothes off the hangers.

'No—wait!'

'No wait. Twenty minutes.'

'But...where am I going?' she asked.

The stylist shrugged, picked up a green-sequinned dress barely larger than a handkerchief, and advanced towards her. Sasha stepped back as the tiny woman waved her hand in front of her.

'Off.'

With a sense of damning inevitability...and more than a little thrill of excitement...she let herself be pulled forward. 'Okay, but definitely not the green.'

The stylist nodded, trilled out an order in Mandarin, and advanced again with another dress.

Twenty minutes later Sasha stepped from the cool, air-conditioned car onto another red carpet. This time, without

Marco, she was even more self-conscious than before. On a warm, sultry Singapore night, the cream silk dress she'd chosen felt more exposing than it had in the safety of her hotel room. At first glance she'd refused to wear the bohemian mini-dress because...well, because it had no back. But then the stylist had fastened the draping material across her lower back and Sasha had felt...*sexy*—like a woman for the first time in her life.

Her hair was fastened with gold lamé rope, her nails polished and glittering. The look was completed with four-inch gold stilettos she'd never dreamt she'd be able to walk in, but she found it surprisingly easy.

Romano appeared at her side, his presence a reminder that somewhere beyond the wild flashes of the paparazzi's cameras Marco was waiting for her.

All the way from her hotel she'd felt the emptiness receding, but had been too scared to acknowledge that Marco had anything to do with it. Now she couldn't stop a smile from forming on her face as the loud boom of fireworks signalled the start of the rock concert.

The VIP lounge teemed with rock stars and pop princesses. She tried to make small talk as she surreptitiously searched the crowd for Marco. Someone thrust a glass of champagne in her hand.

Half an hour later, when a Columbian platinum-selling songstress with snake hips asked who her designer was, Sasha started to answer, then stopped as an ice-cold thought struck her. Was Marco even here? Had she foolishly misinterpreted his note and dressed up only to be stood up?

The depths of her hurt stunned her into silence.

She barely felt any remorse as the pop star flounced off in a huff. Blindly she turned for the exit, humiliation scouring through her.

'Sasha? You're heading for the stage, right?' Tom grabbed her arm and stopped her.

'The...the stage?'

'Your favourite band is about to perform. Marco had me fly them out here just for you.'

'He *what*?' A different kind of *stun* stopped her heart.

'Come on—you don't want them to start without you.'

A thousand questions raced through her brain, but she didn't have time to voice a single one before she was propelled onto the stage and into the arms of the band's lead singer.

Torn between awe at sharing the stage with her favourite band, and happiness that she hadn't misinterpreted Marco's note after all, Sasha knew the next ten minutes were the most surreal of her life. Even seeing herself super-sized on half a dozen giant screens didn't freak her out as much as she'd imagined.

She exited the stage to the crowd's deafening roar. Tom beamed as he helped her down the stairs.

'Have you seen Marco?' Sasha attributed her breathlessness to her onstage excitement—not her yearning to see Marco de Cervantes.

Tom's smile slipped and his gaze dropped. 'Um, he was around a moment ago...'

She told herself not to read anything into Tom's answer. 'Where is he?'

'Sasha...' He sighed and pointed towards the roped-off area manned by three burly bodyguards.

At first she didn't see him, her sight still fuzzy from the bright stage lights.

When she finally focused, when she finally saw what her mind refused to compute, Sasha was convinced her heart had been ripped from her chest.

Each step she took out of the concert grounds felt like a walk towards the opening mouth of a yawning chasm. But Sasha forced herself to keep going, to smile, to acknowledge the accolades and respect she finally had from her team.

Even though inside she was numb and frozen.

The knock came less than ten minutes later.

Marco leaned against the lintel. The buttons of his shirt were *still* undone; his hair was unkempt. As if hands—*female hands*—had run through it several times. He stood there, arrogantly imposing, larger than life.

She hated him more than she could coherently express. And yet the sight of him kicked her heart into her throat.

'What do you want?' she blurted past the pain in her throat.

His gaze, intense and unnerving, left her face to take in the bikini she'd changed into. 'Why did you leave the concert?'

'Why aren't you back there, being pawed by your Italian sexpot?'

'You left because you saw me with Flavia?'

'You know what they say—two's company, three's a flash mob. Now, if you'll excuse me…' She grabbed her kaftan from the bed and the box containing the diamond necklace.

'Here—take this back. I don't want it.'

'It's yours. Every member of the team receives a gift for the team's win. This is yours.'

Her mouth dropped open. 'You're kidding me?'

'I'm not. Where are you going?'

She stared at the box, not sure how to refuse the gift now. 'For a swim—not that it's any of your business.'

'A swim? At this hour?'

'Singapore is the longest race on the calendar. It's even longer when you're leading and trying to defend your position. If I don't warm up and do my stretching exercises my muscles will seize up. That's what I'd planned to do before… Whatever—will you please get out of my way?'

His gaze dropped to her legs. A hoarse sound rumbled from his throat. A look entered his eyes—one that made her excited and afraid at the same time.

'Marco, I said—'

'I heard you.' Still, he didn't move away. Instead, he extracted his phone and issued a terse command in Spanish, his gaze on her the whole time.

Sasha dropped the box on the bed and took a deep calming breath, willing her skin to stop tingling, her heartbeat to slow down. Her senses were too revved up, ready to unleash the full power of her conflicted feelings for this man.

'Let's go.' He finally moved out of the doorway.

'I'm not going anywhere with you until you tell me what you're doing here,' she responded.

He speared a hand through his hair, mussing up the luxurious strands even more. 'Does it matter why I'm here, Sasha? Are you happy to see me?' he demanded in a low, charged tone.

She hated the fire that raced through her veins, stinging her body to painful life in a way even her first race win hadn't been able to achieve.

'Less than half an hour ago you had another woman all over you. Last time I checked, my name wasn't Sloppy Seconds Sasha.'

He swore under his breath. 'You know, you're the most difficult, infuriating woman I know.'

Despite the raspy vehemence in his tone, she smiled. 'Thank you.'

He took her arm and led her to the lift. 'It wasn't a compliment.'

'I know. But I'll take it as one.' She tried not to breathe too deeply of his scent as he stepped in beside her.

The lift whisked them upwards. From the corner of her eye she saw him turn his phone off and shove it into his pocket.

The doors opened onto a space that was so beautiful Sasha couldn't speak for several seconds. In the soft breeze potted palm trees swayed. Strategically placed lights gave the space an exotic but intimate feel that just begged to be enjoyed. Several feet away an endless, boomerang shaped infinity pool poised over the tip of the hotel's tower glimmered blue and silver.

Then she noticed what was missing. 'It's empty.' There wasn't a single soul on the sixtieth-floor skydeck.

'*Sí.*'

The way he responded had her turning to face him.

'You had something to do with it?'

A simple nod.

'Why?'

His shook his head in disbelief. 'That's the hundredth question you've asked since I knocked on your door. I didn't want your swim to be interrupted.'

She kicked away her slippers, her temperature rising another notch when his gaze dropped to her bare feet. 'This pool is three times the size of an Olympic pool. It's hardly cramped.'

His gaze turned molten. 'I wanted privacy.' He released the last button on his shirt and it fell open to reveal a golden washboard torso.

Heat piled on. Beneath the Lycra bikini, her nipples tightened, and her stomach muscles quivered with a need so strong she could barely breathe. 'I see. Will you snarl at me if I ask why?'

'Yes,' he snarled.

Striding to her, he drew the hem of her kaftan over her head and tossed it over his shoulder. Then he took her hair tie, raked his fingers through the strands and secured her hair on top of her head.

Fresh waves of desire threatened to drown her. 'Marco...'

'How many laps do you need to be less tense?'

'Tw—twenty.' She couldn't drag her eyes from the beauty of his face, from the sensual, inviting curve of his mouth.

'Twenty laps it is, then.' He shrugged off his shirt, then released his belt.

Her eyes widened. 'What are you doing?'

'What does it look like?'

'Um...'

Without warning he leaned forward and sniffed the skin between her neck and shoulder. 'You're covered in *eau de* Sleazy Rock Star. I smell of cloying Italian perfume. What say we wash the scent of other people off our skin, and then we'll talk, *si*?

'Marco...'

He swore under his breath. 'Go, Sasha. I need to cool off, or *Dios* help me, I won't be responsible for my actions.'

She went, with the heaviness of his hot gaze scorching her skin.

Pausing at one end of the pool, she stretched her arms over her head. At his sharp intake of breath, she let a sensual smile curve her lips.

The water was a welcome but temporary relief from the sensations arcing between them. He dived in after her a second later, quickly caught up with her and matched her stroke for stroke. When she swam faster, to escape the frenzied need clawing inside, he kept up with her.

His presence made every stroke of water against her skin feel like a caress. At the last lap he increased his pace and heaved himself out of the water. She clung to the side, her lungs heaving, and watched the play of water on his magnificent body as he returned to the poolside.

'Out,' he commanded tersely, his hand holding out a towel like a bull-baiting matador.

She rose out of the pool, careful not to look at the wet clinginess of his boxers. He folded the towel around her, his movements brisk as he rubbed the moisture off her. Then he swung her into his arms and carried her to the enclosed cabana a few feet away.

Two silk-covered loungers stood side by side, separated by a table laid out with several platters of food, from local delicacies to caviar on blinis. In a sterling silver tub a linen-draped bottle of vintage champagne chilled on ice.

Marco set her down on the lounger and picked up the bottle.

Sasha forced her gaze from the play of muscles and looked at the table. 'There's enough here to feed an army.' Reaching for a small plate, she dished out grilled prawns and fragrant rice.

'You don't like caviar?'

She grimaced. 'It smells funny and tastes disgusting. I don't know why people eat the stuff.' She took a mouthful of her food and felt the explosion of textures on her tongue. Thankfully she managed to swallow without choking. 'Now, *this* is heavenly.' She took another mouthful and groaned.

Marco took his seat across from her and held out one glass of champagne, his gaze never leaving hers. What she glimpsed in the heated depths made her heart quicken.

'Marco—'

'Eat. We'll talk when you're done.'

How can I eat? she wanted to ask. Especially when his eyes followed her every move. But words refused to form on her lips.

It was as if he'd cast some sort of spell on her. Maybe he was a vampire after all, she thought hysterically.

The thought should have lightened her mood, made it easier for her to cope, but all it did was cause a fevered shudder to race down her spine.

Clawing in a desperate breath, she set the plate aside. 'Let's talk now. You invited me to the concert, then ignored me to make out with your girlfriend. What else is there to talk about?'

'Flavia's not my girlfriend, and I wasn't making out with her. She was congratulating me on the team's win, just like a lot of people have done tonight.'

'She was *all* over you. And you didn't seem to mind.'

'I was…preoccupied.'

She snorted. 'Evidently.'

'*Para el amor de Dios!* I was waiting in the VIP room for *you*! The Prime Minister turned up when I was about to come and meet you. I tried to get away as quickly as possible, only to find you were more interested in plastering yourself all over your favourite rock star. It was very evident you didn't have a bra on, but tell me—were you even wearing panties under that dress?'

A harsh flush of anger tinged his cheekbones. This was the angriest she'd ever seen Marco. The reason why stopped her breath.

'You were jealous?'

His jaw clenched. 'Do you mean was that what I expected when I had the band flown over for you? No. Did I want to break every bone in his pathetically thin body? *Sí*. For starters.'

The air thickened around them.

A thousand different questions rushed into her mind. One emerged.

'I'm not stupid, Marco, I know where this is going. But what about the consequences? The ones that made you avoid me for the past three weeks?'

He abandoned his glass and rested his hands on his knees, his eyes never leaving hers. 'Seeing you in another man's arms has simplified my decision. For the sake of my sanity, and to avoid murder charges, no more staying away,' he rasped.

'Right. Well, I'm happy for you and your sanity. But what about what *I* want?'

His eyes dropped to her lips. 'If you know where this is going then you know how badly I want to kiss you. Come here.'

Her mouth, the subject of his very intense scrutiny, tingled so badly she had to curb the urge to bite it. 'I meant what I said in London. I don't want a relationship.'

A hard look passed through his eyes. 'I don't want a relationship either.'

'What about *your* clause?'

'I'm not a racing driver and I don't work for the team so I'm exempt. Come here, Sasha.'

'No. Aren't you twisting the rules?'

'No. I can quote them verbatim for you later. Right now I want you to come over here and kiss me.'

Her breath shortened. 'What if I don't want to?'

His gaze darkened. 'Then I'll return to the concert, find your reedy rock star and decorate the VIP lounge with him.'

A roar went up a few miles away. The throb of the rock concert echoed superbly the blood surging through her veins as Marco continued to watch her.

'I hope you won't expect me to bail you out of jail.'

He shrugged. 'I live in hope for a lot of things, *querida*. At this moment I'm hoping you'll stop arguing and crawl into my lap. Would it help if I said that not a day went by these past three weeks when you didn't feature in my thoughts?' He lifted a winged brow.

'Maybe that helps. A little...'

Without warning he reached across the table and scooped her up. Settling her in his lap, he freed her hair and sighed in pleasure as the heavy tresses spilled into his hands. Then he lowered her until her back rested on the upraised lounger.

Despite her bikini's relative modesty, Sasha had never felt more exposed in her life. Especially when Marco took his time to trail his fierce gaze over her, missing nothing as he scoured her body, and followed more slowly with one long, lazy finger.

'You're doing it again.' Her voice was smoky with lust, her flesh alight wherever he touched.

'What?' he murmured, his eyes resting at the apex of her thighs.

Beneath her bottom the hard ridge of his erection pressed into her flesh, its heat making her skin tighten in feverish anticipation.

'The thing with your eyes. And your hands. And your body.'

'If you want me to stop you'll have to kiss me.'

'Maybe I don't want you to stop. Maybe this is what I'll allow before I decide this is a very bad idea.'

His finger paused on her belly. 'You think this is a bad idea?'

A thread of uncertainty wheedled through her desire. 'My last involvement left a lot of bruises.'

He tensed. 'Derek physically hurt you?'

'No, but he influenced a lot of people against me. You included.'

He shook his head. 'I make up my own mind. If you truly don't want this, say the word and I'll stop.'

The thought of denying herself made her heart lurch painfully.

Her body moved closer of its own volition. He hissed out a breath, the skin around his mouth tightening as he visibly reined in control. 'If you intend to stop that's not a great idea, *querida*.'

Sasha had had enough. Marco had spent far too much of his life controlling everything. For once she yearned to see him lose his cool, to crack the shell of tightly reined-in emotion. She wriggled again.

His gaze connected with hers. The dark hunger in its depths made her breath catch. Giving in to the urge, she slipped her hand over his nape and urged his head down.

He took control of her lips in a kiss so driven, so desperate, she cried out against his mouth. He fisted one hand in her hair to hold her still, his other hand sliding over her bottom to drag her closer.

Sasha went willingly, her body a fluid vessel of rampant desire that craved only him. Every single doubt that crowded in her brain drowned under ever-increasing waves of sensation.

She might be risking everything to experience a few hours of pleasure, but Sasha could no more push Marco away than she could voluntarily stop breathing. She would deal with regret in the morning.

Losing herself in the kiss, she boldly thrust her tongue against his. His body jerked, making a tiny fizz of pleasure steal through her.

When his fingers squeezed her buttock, she moaned.

He pulled back. 'You like that?' he rasped, his gaze heavy and hooded.

She nodded and licked her lips, already missing the feel of his mouth against hers.

'Tell me what else you'd like, *mi tentación*.' He released the tie of her bikini top and trailed his mouth over her skin.

'You…not to be so overdressed…' she gasped out.

Another roar from the concert ripped through the night air. Momentarily she remembered where they were.

'On the other hand, maybe that's not so bad—'

'We won't be disturbed.'

The finality of the statement, along with the graze of his teeth over one Lycra-clothed nipple, melted the last of her reservations. Giving her feelings free rein, she slid her hand over his shoulders, touching the smooth skin of his nape before exploring his damp, luxurious hair.

Her urgency fed his. With renewed vigour he kissed her again, pulling off the wet cloth and tossing it aside. Reversing their positions, he eased her onto the lounger, then tugged off her bikini bottoms.

In the soft, ambient light of the enclosed cabana his skin gleamed golden, the dark silky hairs on his chest making her fingers tingle to touch.

'I want to touch you all over.' The heated words had slipped out before she could stop them.

His face contorted in a pained grimace. Tugging off his boxers, he stretched out next to her. Leaning down, he ran his tongue over her mouth. 'I believe I mentioned the near insanity that has plagued me these past weeks? Touching me all over is not a good idea right now.'

Her breath rasped through her chest. Breathing had become increasingly difficult. 'Oh. Then I guess it's not a good time to mention I also intend biting a few strategic places?'

A heartfelt groan preceded a few heated Spanish words muttered against her lips. 'Do me a favour, *mi tentadora*. Keep your thoughts to yourself for the time being. You have my word. I'll let you vocalise your every want later.'

Swooping down, he captured one exposed nipple in his mouth, his fierce determination to shut her up working wonders. Words deserted her as sensation took over. Liquid heat pooled at the apex of her thighs, the flesh of her sex swelling and pulsating with the strength of her need. By the time he transferred his attention to her other nipple Sasha was incoherent with desire.

Marco traced his lips lower, ruthlessly turning her inside out with pleasure, but when she felt his mouth dip below her navel she froze.

Sensing her withdrawal, he raised his head. 'You don't want this?'

'I *do*.' So much so the force of her need shocked her. 'I do... But you don't have to if...' Her words fizzled out at the searing heat in his eyes.

'I've spent endless nights imagining the taste of you, Sasha.' He parted her legs wider, licked the sensitive skin inside her thigh, his eyes growing darker at her breathless groan. 'But I've always preferred reality to dreams.'

He put his mouth on her, slowly worked his tongue over the millions of nerve-endings saturated with pleasure receptors. Sasha screamed, and came in a rush of pleasure so intense her whole body quivered with it.

Before the last of her orgasm had faded away Marco was surging over her. His kiss was less frantic but no less demanding. And, just like the engine of a finely tuned car, her body responded to his demands, anticipation firing her blood like nothing had ever done in her life.

Tension screamed through Marco's body as he raised himself from the intoxicating kiss. The sound of Sasha's orgasm echoed in his head like a siren's call, promising him pleasure beyond measure. He couldn't remember ever being so fired up about sex—so impatient he'd nearly forgotten protection.

Luckily sanity prevailed just in time.

Sasha moved restlessly beneath him, her sultry gaze steady on his as he parted her thighs.

Every single night of the past three weeks he'd woken with an ache in his groin and a sinking sensation that he was fighting a losing battle. He'd congratulated himself on staying away, but he'd known deep down it was a hollow victory.

Truth was he'd never wanted a woman as much as he wanted Sasha. He'd stopped trying to decipher what made her so irresistible. She just *was*. He'd also made discreet enquiries and verified that she'd spoken the truth—she hadn't been involved with Rafael.

So just this once he was going to take. Sasha Fleming had worked her way under his skin like no other woman had and now this was the inevitable conclusion. Her underneath him, her thighs parted, her sultry gaze steady on his. Just as he'd dreamed...

With a groan he sank into her.

'Thank God!' she cried. 'For a second there I thought you were about to change your mind.'

As if to stop him taking that route, her muscles clamped tight around him.

Another groan tore from his throat. 'I thought I told you to shut up?' He pulled back and surged into her once more, pleasure such as he'd never known rocking through him.

'I am... I will... Just please don't stop.' Raking her nails down his back, she clamped her hands around his waist.

As if he could even if he wanted to. He was past the point of no return, his need so great he was almost afraid to acknowledge its overwhelming scope. Instead he lost himself in her pleasure, in the hitched sounds and feminine demands of her body as she welcomed him into her sweet warmth.

'*Dios*, you feel incredible,' he rasped as sensation piled upon sensation.

Inevitably the bough broke. Ecstasy rode through him, blinding him to everything else but the glorious satisfaction of unleashed passion.

With her cry of bliss he followed off the peak, the muscles in his body tightening with the force of his orgasm as he emptied himself into her.

He collapsed on top of her, her soft, sweat-slicked body a cushion to his hardness. He remained there until their breathing calmed then, rolling onto the lounger, he tucked her against his side.

As the last of the haze faded away he felt the first inevitable twinge of regret. He'd succumbed to temptation. Now the piper would expect payment. And for the first time in his life Marco was afraid at just how much he was willing to pay.

CHAPTER NINE

'WHAT—?' Sasha jerked awake.

The solid body curved around hers and the arm imprisoning her kept her from falling off the lounger. Opening her eyes, she encountered Marco's accusing gaze.

'You fell asleep.'

The wide expanse of muscled chest scrambled her brain for a few seconds, before a few synapses fired a thought. She'd had sex with Marco. Wild, unbelievable, pleasure-filled sex. After which—

'You fell *asleep*,' he incised a second time, affront stamped all over his face.

'Uh...I'm sorry...'

'I get the feeling you don't mean that.'

'And I get the feeling I'm not following this conversation at all.' Before she could stop it a wide yawn broke through.

His glare darkened.

'Did I not please you?' He seemed genuinely puzzled, and a little unsure. One hand curved under her nape to tilt her face up to his.

Thoughts of their lovemaking melted her insides. 'Of course you did,' she said, struggling to keep from blushing at recalling her cries of pleasure. Lifting her hands, she framed his face. 'I've never felt more pleasure than I did with you.'

'It was so good you fell asleep straight after?'

'Take it as a compliment. You wore me out.'

His lids veiled his eyes. 'This is a first, I admit.'

'Wearing a woman out?' she asked, stunned.

'Of course not. The falling asleep part.'

Laughter bubbled up from deep within her, delight filling her. Leaning up, she pressed her lips against his in a light kiss.

Marco took over and turned it into a long, deep kiss.

By the time he was done with her she struggled to breathe. And he…he was fully engorged, his erection a forceful presence against her belly. Emboldened by the thought that she could arouse him again so quickly, she caressed her fingers down his side, eliciting a shuddered groan from him that released a wanton smile from her.

'Like I said, I'm sorry. How can I make it up to you?' She slid her hand between them and gripped him tight. His lips parted on another groan. She caressed up and down, marvelling at the tensile strength of him.

His mouth trailed over her face to the juncture between her neck and shoulder. Erotic heat washed through her.

When her grip tightened, his breath shuddered out. '*Sí, mi querida*, that's the right way to make it up to me.'

His hips bucked against her hold, heat and strength pulsing through her fingers. Liquid heat gathered between her thighs. She was unbelievably turned on by the pleasure she gave him.

At yet another caress he suddenly reared up and flipped her over. 'You're getting carried away.'

She slid her thighs either side of him and lowered herself until her wet heat touched him. The feel of his strong hands sliding down her back to capture her bottom made her shiver with delight.

'Then me being on top wasn't the best idea, was it?'

His predatory gaze swept over her, lingering on her breasts, making them peak even more painfully.

'It's time you learned that I can control you from whichever position I'm in,' he breathed.

He surged into her, filling her so completely stars exploded behind her closed lids. He captured her nape, forced her down and took her mouth in a scorching kiss. His tongue seeking the deep cavern of her mouth, he took her over completely, escalating the desire firing through her until Sasha was aflame with a pleasure so intense it frightened the small part of her brain that could still function.

Sasha hung on as he clamped one hand in the small of her back to hold her still. His pace was frantic, frightful in its demand and exquisite in its delivery of pleasure. She whimpered when he freed her mouth, only to blindly seek his for herself before she could draw another breath. Sensation spiralled out of control as bliss gathered with stunning speed.

'Open your eyes. Let me see your eyes when you come for me.'

She obeyed. Then wished she hadn't when the heat in his eyes threatened to send her already flaming world out of control.

'Marco…'

'*Sí*, I feel it too.'

She believed him. The sheen of sweat coating his skin, the unsteady hand that caressed down her face before recapturing her nape, the harsh pants that escaped his lungs all attested to the fact that he was caught in this incredible maelstrom too.

Pleasure scythed through her heart, arrowed down into her pelvis, forcing her to cry out one last time as her orgasm exploded through her.

Beneath her, still controlling their pleasure, Marco thrust into her release, groaning at the sensation of her caressing convulsions, then found his own satisfaction.

Their harsh breaths mingled, hearts thundering as the breeze cooled their sweat-damp skin. Far away, another burst of fireworks lit up the sky.

Inside the cabana, the intensity of their shared pleasure sparked a threat of fear through her.

To mask her feelings, she hid her face in his shoulder. 'I'd love to compose a sonnet to you right now. But I have no words.'

A short rumble of laughter echoed through his heated chest. 'Sonnets are overrated. Your screams of pleasure were reward enough.'

Sasha sighed, put her head on his chest and tried to breathe. The alarm that had taken root in that small part of her brain grew. Something had happened between their first and second lovemaking.

Then she'd felt safe enough to fall asleep in Marco's arms.

Now... Now she felt exposed. Her emotions felt raw, naked. Unbidden, tears prickled her eyes. She scrambled to hide her composure but Marco sensed her feelings.

Pushing her head gently off his shoulder, he stared into her face. 'You're crying. Why?'

How could she explain something she had no understanding of?

When she tried to shrug he shook his head. 'Tell me.'

'I'm just feeling a little overwhelmed. That's all.'

After a second he nodded and brushed a hand down her cheek. '*Sí.* This is your first victory. That feeling can never be equalled.'

For several heartbeats Sasha didn't follow his meaning. When she realised he was talking about the race, and not the roiling aftermath of their lovemaking, her heart lurched.

Panic escalating, she grasped the lifeline. 'I wish my father had been there.'

Marco nodded. 'He would've been proud of you.'

Surprise widened her eyes. 'You knew my father?'

'Of course. He was the greatest driver never to win a championship. I've seen every single race of his. Clearly you inherited his talent.'

The unexpected compliment made her feel even more tearful. She tried to move away but he caught her back easily, lowered his head and kissed his way along her arm. When she shivered, he shook out a cashmere throw and pulled it over them, one muscular leg imprisoning both of hers.

She was grateful for the cover—not least because the familiar feeling of humiliation had returned. 'You know what happened to him, then?'

'He bet on another car to win and deliberately crashed his car.' The cold conviction in his voice sent an icy shiver down her spine, bleeding away the warmth she'd felt in his arms.

This time she moved away forcefully. Standing, she grabbed

her kaftan and slid it over her head, even though it did little to cover her nakedness.

'The allegations were false!'

Marco folded his arms behind his head. 'Not according to the court that found him guilty.'

'He never managed to disprove the claims. But *I* believed him. He would *never* have done that. He loved racing too much to crash deliberately for money.'

'I was on the board that reviewed the footage, Sasha. The evidence was hard to refute.'

Shock and anger twisted in her gut. '*You* were one of those who decided he was guilty?'

He lowered his feet to the floor. 'He didn't do much to defend himself. It took him weeks to even acknowledge the charges.'

'And that makes him automatically guilty? He was devastated! Yes, he should have responded to the allegations earlier, but the accusations broke his heart.'

Her voice choked as memories rushed to the fore. Her father broken, disgraced by the sport he'd devoted his life to. It had taken Sasha weeks to convince her father to fight to clear his name. And in those precious weeks his reputation in the eyes of the public had been sullied beyond repair. By the time Jack Fleming had taken the stand his integrity had been in tatters.

'So he gave up? And let you carry the weight of his guilt?'

'Of course not!'

'Why did you promise him the championship?'

Sasha floundered, pain and loss ripping through her. 'He started drinking heavily after the trial. The only time he stopped was when I had a shot at the Formula Two Championship. When I crashed and had to stay a while in hospital he started drinking again.'

'You were in hospital? And the father you claim loved you *unconditionally* wasn't there for you?'

Hazel eyes now devoid of passion taunted her.

Tears prickled her eyes but she refused to let them fall. In her darkest, most painful moments after losing her baby she'd asked herself the same question.

Blinking fiercely, she raised her chin. 'Whatever point you're trying to make, Marco, make it without being a total bastard.'

He sighed and ran a hand over his chin.

She stayed at the other end of the cabana, her arms curved around her middle.

'Did you hire another lawyer to appeal?'

'Of course we did. He... Dad died before the second trial.'

His gaze softened a touch. 'How did he die?'

'He drove his car off a bridge near our cottage.' Pain coated her words. 'Everyone thinks he did it because he was guilty. He was just...devastated.'

'And you feel guilty for this?'

She plucked at the hem of her kaftan. 'If I hadn't got involved with Derek I'd have won a championship earlier. Maybe that would've saved my father...'

Marco's hand slashed through her words. 'Your life is your own. You can't live it for someone else. Not even your father.'

'Who's got their psychoanalysing hat on now?'

His brow lifted. 'You can dish it out but you can't take it?'

Sasha tried to stem the wave of guilt that rose within her. After his trial she'd suggested her father not come to her races, because she'd watched him slide deeper into depression after attending every one.

'Whatever he was, he wasn't a cheat. And I intend to honour his memory.'

Marco rose from the lounger, completely oblivious to his sheer masculine beauty and the effect it had on her tangled emotions. Sasha wanted to burrow into him, to return to the warm cocoon of his arms. But she forced herself to stay where she was.

'Come here.'

She shook her head. 'No. I don't like you very much right now.'

His smile made a mockery of her words as he strolled towards her. 'That's not true. You can't keep your eyes off me. Just like I can't take mine off you.'

'Marco...'

He cupped her jaw and lifted her face to his. Her heart stuttered, then thundered. 'You made your promise out of guilt—'

'No, I want to win the Championship.'

'Sometimes the best deal is to walk away.'

'I don't intend to. So don't stand in my way.'

He brought his mouth within a whisper of hers. Sasha swayed towards him, her willpower depleting rapidly.

'Determination is a quality I admire, *querida*. But remember I won't tolerate anything that stands in the way of *my* desires.'

Tugging her firmly into his arms, he proceeded to make her forget everything but him. Including the fact that he'd never believed her father's innocence.

Marco attended the next two races, flying back each time from Spain, where Rafael was still in a coma. When she won in Japan he took the whole team to celebrate, after which he took Sasha to his penthouse for a private celebration of their own.

After a tricky, hair-raising start, Korea secured her yet another victory. But one look at Marco's taut expression when she emerged from the press conference told her there would be no team celebrations this time.

'Marco?'

'We're leaving. Now.'

He whisked her away from the Yeongam Circuit in his helicopter, his possessive fingers tense around hers all through the flight to a stunning beach house on the outskirts of Seoul City, where he proceeded to strip off her race suit and her underclothes.

'You know that by dragging me away like that in front of the team you've blown this thing between us wide open, don't you?' she asked, in the aftermath of another pulse-melting session in his bed.

His lovemaking had been especially intense, with an edge that had bordered on the frenzied. And, as much as she'd loved it, he'd left her struggling for breath, in danger of being swept away by the force of his passion.

He brushed a damp curl from her cheek and studied her face. 'Does it bother you?'

She gave the matter brief thought. 'There was speculation even before we were together. Paddock gossip can make the tabloid press look like amateurs.'

He pulled back slightly, his earlier tension returning. 'That doesn't answer my question.'

'They knew I was a good driver before I started sleeping with you. They just didn't want to acknowledge it because of who I am. I only care about what they think of me as a driver. What they think of me personally doesn't matter. It never has.'

'You're a fighter,' he said, his expression reflective.

'I've had to fight for what I've achieved.' She cast him a droll look. 'As you well know.'

When he didn't smile back, a cloud appeared on the horizon of her happy haze. 'It bothers you that I don't care what other people think about me?'

'Single-mindedness has its place.'

'I smell a *but* in there somewhere.'

His gaze because suspiciously neutral. 'Following a single dream is risky. When it's taken from you you'll have nothing.'

'*When?* Not *if*? Are you trying to tell me something?'

'Nothing lasts for ever.'

'You must be jet-lagged again, because you've gone all cryptic on me. I'm three races away from securing the Constructors' Championship for you. Unless I don't finish another single race, and our nearest rival wins every one, it's pretty much a done deal.'

He got out of bed and pulled on his boxer shorts. For a man who embraced nudity the way Marco did, the definitive action sent a shiver of unease down her spine.

'Done deals have a way of coming undone.'

Her anxiety escalated. 'Enough with the paradoxes. What's going on, Marco?'

Marco strode to the champagne chilling in a monogrammed silver bucket, filled up a glass and brought it back to her.

Returning to the cabinet, he poured a whisky for himself and downed it in one go.

He slammed the glass down and spun towards her. '*Madre di Dios*, you nearly crashed today!'

Her fingers tightened around the delicate stem of her glass as the full force of his smouldering temper hit her. Her car had stalled at the start of the race, leaving her struggling to retain pole position. Her rivals hadn't hesitated in trying to take advantage of the situation. She'd touched tyres with a couple of cars and nearly lost a front wing.

'I found myself in a slightly hairy situation. I dealt with it.' She glanced at him. 'Were you worried?'

'That my lover would end up in a mangled heap of metal just like my brother did mere weeks ago? What do you think?' he ground out.

She trembled at the harshness in his tone even while a secret part of her thrilled that he'd been worried about her. 'I know what I'm doing, Marco. I've been doing it almost all my life.'

He speared a hand into her hair, tilting her face up to his. 'Rafael knew what he was doing too. Look where he ended up. You can't do it for ever. You do realise that, don't you?'

The question threw her, for Sasha had been deliberately avoiding any thoughts of the future. Even the end of the racing season didn't bear thinking about. If by some sheer stroke of bad luck she lost the Constructors' Championship then she was out of a job.

If she won her professional future would be secured for another year. But what about her personal future?

The reality was that she'd fallen into Marco's bed expecting little more than a one-night stand. But with each day that passed she was being consumed by the magic she experienced there. With no thought to the future…

'Yes,' she finally whispered. 'I realise nothing lasts for ever.'

'*Bueno*,' he breathed, as if her answer had satisfied him.

He shucked his boxers in one smooth move. 'Are you going to drink that? Only, after watching you nearly crash, I feel an urgent need to re-affirm life with you again. Repeatedly.'

She passed him the glass and opened her arms.

It wasn't until their breaths were gasping out in the aftermath of soul-shattering orgasms that she tensed in disbelief.

'Marco!'

'What?' He raised his head, a swathe of hair falling seductively over one eye.

'We didn't... We forgot...' Frantically she calculated dates.

He let loose a single epithet. '*Dios.* Please tell me you're on the Pill?' he rasped.

His voice was a choked sound that chilled her.

Reassured with the dates, she nodded, then noticed his pallor. 'Hey, it's okay. Even if the Pill doesn't work it's the wrong time of the month.'

'Are you sure?' he demanded.

Frowning, Sasha laid a hand on his cheek, which had grown cold and clammy. 'I'm sure. Relax.'

Marco eased away from Sasha, steeling himself against her throaty protest as he left the bed. Pulling on a robe, he went into his study. His laptop was set up on his desk, his folders neatly arranged by his assistant. He bypassed it, threw himself into the leather sofa and scrubbed a hand down his face.

He hadn't meant to lose it with Sasha like that earlier.

But seeing her come within a whisker of crashing had set him on a knife-edge of fear and rage he hadn't been able to completely dismiss. Now his loss of control had made him forget his one cardinal rule—contraception. *Always.*

He hadn't slipped once in ten years. Until tonight. Thank goodness Sasha was as against accidentally conceiving a child as he was...

Grimly reining in the control that seemed to be slipping from him, he strode to his desk and picked up the top folder. A sliver of guilt rose inside him but he quashed it.

Enough. He'd done what needed to be done. He refused to feel guilty for protecting what was important to him. Nothing mattered except keeping his family safe.

He picked up the phone and called his brother's doctors. Once he'd been updated on Rafael's condition, he placed another call.

Fifteen minutes later he slammed down the lid of his laptop and pushed away from the desk, at peace with his decision.

Feeling a sense of rightness, he returned to the bedroom and slid into bed, his need for Sasha overcoming the wish to let her rest. With a soft murmur she wound her supple body around his. The sense of rightness increased, making his head spin.

'I missed you. Where have you been?'

Another wave of guilt hit him—harder than before. Inhaling the seductive scent of her, he pushed away the disturbing feeling. 'I needed to take care of something.' Bending his head, he placed his lips against the smooth skin of her neck. His body stirred, transmitting its persistent message.

'Um. And have you?' she murmured.

'*Sí.*' His voice emerged gruffer than he wished. 'It's all taken care of.'

CHAPTER TEN

SASHA watched Marco turn the page of his newspaper, a frown creasing his brow before it smoothed out again. Watching him had become something of a not-so-secret pleasure in the last few weeks. On cue, she experienced the slow drag of desire in her belly as her gaze drifted over the sensual curve of his lips, the unshaven rasp of his jaw and the strong column of his throat to the muscled bare torso which she'd caressed to her heart's content last night and this morning.

As if sensing her gaze, his eyes met hers over the top of the paper. One brow lifted. 'You want to go back to bed?'

He laughed at her less-than-convincing shake of the head. The remnants of breakfast lay scattered on the table, long forgotten as they basked in the South Korean sun.

'I didn't know you could read Korean,' she said, eager for something to distil the suffocating heat of the desire that was never far from the surface.

Marco smiled and folded away the paper. 'It's Japanese. I never quite mastered Korean.'

'Wow. You're freely admitting *another* flaw? Shocking!'

He shrugged. 'It was down to a choice of which was the most useful.'

She wrinkled her nose. '*Useful?* Do you ever do anything just for pleasure?'

His droll look made her colour rise higher.

'Besides sex,' she mumbled.

'Sex with you is all the pleasure I crave, *mi corazón.*'

'You have other interests, surely? Everyone does.'

His throaty laugh made her pulse pound harder. 'What did you have in mind?'

'Some culture. An exhibition. Something other than...' Flustered, she waved her hand towards the severely rumpled bed beyond the sliding doors leading into the master suite, trying not to think of all the *other* places—the highly polished teak floor, the wooden bench in his outdoor bathroom, the hammock overlooking the stunning beach—where Marco had pleasured her during the long night.

Leaning over, he slid a hand around her nape and pulled her in for a hot kiss. 'I'd much rather spend the day with you in my bed. But if you insist—'

'I insist.'

Because Sasha had woken up this morning with a fearful knowledge deep in her heart. She was in danger of developing feelings for Marco de Cervantes. Feelings that she dared not name. Feelings that threatened to overwhelm her the more time she spent locked in his embrace.

At least away from this place, real life would impede long enough to knock some sense into her. To remind her that she couldn't afford to lose her head over a man like Marco—a man whom she knew deep down grappled with his guilt for being attracted to her. After all, hadn't it taken him three weeks to decide he could be with her?

He was also a man who believed her father to be guilty of fraud, a small voice added.

A sharp pang pierced through the concrete she'd packed around her pain. She hadn't been able to raise the subject with Marco since that night in Singapore. Somehow knowing he'd painted her father with the same brush of guilt as everyone else hurt so much more. Which made her a fool. Why should he believe any differently? Just because they were sleeping together it didn't mean the taint of her name had disappeared.

'You have fifteen minutes to get ready.'

She roused herself to find Marco ending a call. 'Ready for what?'

He tossed his phone on the table and brushed his knuckle along her jaw. Sparks of pleasure lit along her skin.

'You want culture, *mi encantadora*. Korea awaits.'

'Oh, my God,' Sasha whispered as her bare feet touched the wet flagstones that led to the ancient lake temple, unable to tear her gaze away from the magnificent vista before her.

'I'm finding that I don't like you using that expression unless it relates directly to me, *pequeña*,' Marco complained, releasing her hand as she leapt onto the next flagstone.

'Are you jealous?' she asked on a laugh.

He raised a mocking brow. 'Of your insane adoration of old temples and ancient monuments?' He rolled up his trouser cuffs and stepped on to the flagstones, bringing his warmth and addictive body up close and personal. 'Not a chance. But I suggest you alter your phraseology, because every time you say *Oh, my God* in that sexy tone I want to flatten you against the nearest surface and have my way with you.'

He grinned at her gasp and his head started to descend.

'No.' She pulled away reluctantly.

He frowned. *'Qué diablos?'*

'Shh, we're in a holy place,' she whispered. 'No kissing. And no swearing.'

She giggled at his muted growl and skipped over the rest of the flagstones until she stood in front of the temple.

'Wow.'

'*Wow* I can live with.'

'You'll have to. I have no other words.'

From where they stood the small temple seemed to float on the water, its curved eaves reminiscent of a bird in flight. In the light of the dying sun huge pink water lilies glowed red, their rubescent petals unfurled to catch the last of the sun's rays.

'It's all so beautiful. So stunning.' With reverent steps Sasha approached the temple doors. 'Can we go in?'

He nodded. 'It's not normally open to visitors. But on this occasion…'

Unbidden, a lump rose to her throat. 'Thank you.'

'*De nada.* Go—explore to your heart's content.'

With legs that felt shaky, and a heart that hammered far too hard to be healthy, Sasha paused to wipe her feet, then entered the temple.

Like every single place Marco had taken her to since he'd summoned his car after breakfast, the temple was breathtakingly exquisite. The *shoji* scrolls lining the walls looked paper-thin and fragile, causing her to hold her breath in case she damaged the place in any way. Examining one, she wished she had a translator to explain the three lines of symbols to her.

'"Peace through wisdom. Wisdom through perspicacity,"' Marco murmured from behind her. 'This temple was originally Japanese. It changed owners a few times before the Shaolin monks took over in the fourth century.'

'It puts everything into perspective, doesn't it?'

'Does it?'

'You said nothing lasts for ever. This temple proves some things do.'

For a long moment he didn't answer. His hooded gaze held hers, but in the gathering dusk she couldn't read the expression in his eyes.

'Come, it is time to leave. Romano will think you've kidnapped me.'

'What? Little ol' me?'

He laughed—a sound she was finding she liked very much. 'Romano knows you have a black belt in Jujitsu.'

'I'd still think twice before I tried to drop-kick a man of his size. So you're safe with me.'

'Gracias.' He threaded his fingers through hers, then signalled to Romano to bring the car round.

She waited until they were in the car before leaning over to press her lips to his. 'Thank you for showing me Seoul.'

His hand tightened around her waist and pulled her closer. 'The tour isn't over yet. I have one last treat for you.'

Pleasure unfurled through her. 'Really?'

'The night is just beginning. I know a little place where, if you're really nice to the staff, they'll name a dish after you.

Will you allow me to show it to you?' He picked up her hand
and kissed the back of it.

Watching the dark head bent over her hand, Sasha experienced that irrational fear again. Only this time it was ten times
worse. Her heart hammered and her pulse raced through her
veins as the reason for her feelings whispered softly through
her mind.

No. She *wasn't* falling for Marco de Cervantes. Because that
would be stupid.

And reckless.

Marco didn't do relationships. And she'd barely survived
being burned once.

His lips caressed the sensitive skin of her wrist.

At her helpless sigh, he smiled. 'On second thoughts, a
Michelin-star-chef-prepared meal on the beach sounds very
appealing.'

Resisting temptation was nearly impossible. But Sasha forced
herself to speak. 'It's not fair to dangle the opportunity to have
a dish named after me and then withdraw it. Now it's on my
lust-have list.'

He reached out and cupped her breast. 'I have only one thing
on *my* lust-have list.'

'You're insatiable,' she breathed, unable to stop her moan
when his thumb passed over her nipple.

Bending his head, he brought his lips close to hers. 'Only for
you do I have this need,' he muttered thickly. 'And, *por favor*, I
won't have it denied.' He drew closer until their breaths mingled.

'What about dinner...the dish...?' she whispered.

'You'll have it,' he vowed. 'Just...later.'

With a muted groan, he closed the gap, sealing them in a hot
cocoon of fevered need so intense it stopped her breath.

The cocoon held them intimately all the way through their
torrid lovemaking in Marco's bed and in the shower afterwards,
where he explored every inch of her body as if seeing it for the
first time.

His phone rang as they dressed for dinner. At first she thought
it was a business call. Then she noticed his ashen pallor.

Their cocoon had been shattered.

'Who was that?' she asked, even though part of her knew the answer.

'It was the hospital. Rafael's suffered another bleed.'

'What the hell are you doing under there? Freebasing engine oil?'

Sasha froze at the voice she hadn't heard in six long sleepless nights and forced herself to breathe. 'Hand me the wrench.'

'Didn't the staff tell you no one's allowed in here?' The harsh censure in his voice grated on her already severely frayed nerves.

'They probably *tried*.'

'You didn't listen, of course?'

'I don't speak Spanish, remember? Are you going to hand me the wrench or not?'

His designer-shod feet moved, then a wrench appeared underneath the body of the 1954 Fiat 8V Berlinetta.

'Not that one. The retractable.'

The right wrench reappeared. 'Thanks.'

She hooked the wrench on to the bolt and pulled. Nothing happened.

'Come out from under there.'

'No.'

'Sasha…' His voice held more than a hint of warning.

Her mouth compressed. She didn't want to see his face, didn't want to breathe his scent. In fact she wanted to deny herself everything to do with Marco. To deny that every single atom of her being yearned to wheel herself from under the car and throw herself into his arms.

She gripped the wrench and yanked harder, reminding herself of how almost a week ago he'd ordered Romano to bring her to *Casa de Leon* and walked away.

As if Seoul had never happened.

'We need to talk.'

Her heart clenched. 'So talk.'

An expensively cut suit jacket landed a few feet from her head, followed a millisecond later by Marco's large, tightly packed frame.

'What are you doing?' she squeaked, holding herself rigid as his shoulder brushed hers.

He ignored her, taking his time to study the axle she'd been working on. 'Hand me the wrench and move over.'

'Why? Because you think you're bigger and stronger than me?'

'I *am* bigger and stronger than you.'

'Sexist pig.'

'Simple truth.'

'I see you still live in the Dark Ages.'

'Only when it comes to protecting what's mine.'

Realising he wasn't going to go away, she shrugged. 'Fine. Knock yourself out.'

His gaze sharpened. 'No arguments, *querida*? That's how it works between us usually, isn't it? I say something, then you argue my words to death until I kiss you to shut you up?'

'I don't crave arguments—or your kisses, if that's what you're implying. In fact I'd love nothing better than for you to leave me alone,' she suggested. 'You've managed it quite successfully for almost a week.'

Silently he held out his hand. She slapped the wrench into his palm. With a few firm twists he loosened the bolt on the axle.

'Show-off,' she quipped. 'What do you want?'

'I thought you'd want an update on Rafael.' His gaze stayed intense on hers.

'I thought he was off-limits?'

'If I still believed you and he were involved I wouldn't have taken you to my bed.'

'Okay. So how is he?'

'He's doing better. The doctors managed to stop the bleed. They expect him to wake up any day now.'

Licking her lips carefully, she nodded. 'That's great news.'

'*Sí.*'

The intensity in his eyes sent a bolt of apprehension through her. Without warning, his gaze dropped to her lips. Belatedly Sasha realised she was licking them. She stopped. But the quickening was already happening. The cramped space underneath the car became smaller. The air grew thinner.

'You didn't have to come back here to tell me that. A simple phone call would've sufficed. I'll pack my things and leave this afternoon.'

He stiffened. 'Why would you do that?'

'Rafael will need you when he comes home. I can't be here.'

'Of course you can. I want you here.'

Despite the thin hope threading its way through her, she forced herself to speak. 'That wasn't the impression I got from your six-day silence.'

He sucked in a weary breath and for the first time she noticed the lines of strain around his eyes.

'I didn't expect to be away this long. I'm sorry.'

When her mouth dropped open in surprise at the ready apology he grimaced.

'I know. I must be losing my touch.' He glanced around, his strained look intensifying. 'How did you get in here? The door is combination locked.'

'Rosario let me in. She recognises stir-craziness when she sees it. So—twenty-five vintage cars locked away in a garage? Discuss.'

He inhaled sharply, then flung the wrench away. 'I refuse to have this conversation underneath a car, with grease dripping on me.'

'You should've thought of that before you crawled down here.'

'*Dios*, I've missed your insufferable attitude.' He paused. 'This is your chance to tell me you've missed me too.'

The stark need to do just that frightened her. 'Are you sure you don't want me to leave? I can go home for a few days before the team leaves for Abu Dhabi next week. Maybe it's for the best.'

'And maybe you need to shut up. Just for one damn moment,' he snarled, then grabbed her arm and turned her into his body.

The heat of his mouth devoured hers. Fiery sensation was instantaneous. Sasha held nothing back. Her fingers gripped his nape, luxuriating in the smooth skin before spearing upward to spread through his hair. His deep groan echoed hers. Willingly, she let her mouth fall open, let his tongue invade to slide deliciously against hers.

His hand snaked around her waist and veered downwards, bringing her flush against his heated body. Need flooded her. To be this close again with him, to feel him, to be with him, made her body, her heart sing.

She wanted to be close. Closer. Physically and emotionally. Because... Because...

Infinitely glad he'd shed his jacket, she explored the large expanse of his shoulders.

When the demands of oxygen forced them apart his gaze stayed on her. One hand cupped her bottom. Against her belly she felt the ripe force of his erection.

'You do realise we're making out under a car, don't you?' she asked huskily.

'It's the only thing stopping me from pulling you on top of me and burying myself inside you. Tell me you missed me.'

'I missed you.'

'Bueno.' He fastened his mouth to hers once more.

By the time he freed her and pulled them from underneath the car her brain had become a useless expanse seeking only the pleasure he could provide. When he undressed her, led her to the back door of a 1938 Rolls-Royce, she was a willing slave, ready to do his every bidding.

Snagging an arm around her waist, he speared a hand through her hair and tilted her face to his. 'You have no idea how long I've wanted to do this.'

'What?' she breathed.

His mouth swooped, locked on the juncture where her shoulder met her neck, where her pulse thundered frantically.

Her blood surged to meet his mouth. When his teeth grazed her skin she cried out. The eroticism of it was so intense that liquid heat pooled between her legs, where she throbbed, plumping up for the studied and potent possession only he could deliver.

He took his time, tasted her, his mouth playing over the delicate, intensely aroused skin. Just when she thought it couldn't get any more pleasurable his tongue joined in. Ecstasy lashed at her insides, creating a path of fire from her neck to her breasts, to her most sensitive part and down to her toes. Nowhere was safe from the utter bliss rushing through her.

Finally, satisfied, he lifted his head. He took a step forward, then another, until the edge of the car seat touched her calves. With his gentle push she fell back onto the wide seat.

He followed immediately, his warmth surrounding her. In his arms she felt delicate, cared for, as if she mattered. As if she was precious. Which was silly. For Marco this was just sex. But for her...

She shut her mind off the painful train of thought. 'I thought you wanted me on top?'

His teeth gleamed in a slow, feral smile. 'In good time, *mi tentación*. We have a long way to go. Now, don't move.'

He cupped her breasts, toying with the nipples, torturing her for so long she wriggled with pleasure.

'I said don't move,' he gritted through clenched teeth, the harsh stamp of desire tautening his face.

'You expect me to just lie here like a ten-dollar hooker?'

Despite the intense desire threatening to swallow them whole, laughter rumbled through his chest. 'Never having been graced with the attentions of a ten-dollar hooker, I can't answer that. But if you don't stop tormenting me with your body I won't be responsible for my actions.'

'Oh, *now* you're just threatening me with a good time.'

'*Dios*, woman. Your mouth...'

'You want to kiss it?' It was more of a plea than a question. Her head rose off the seat in search of his.

He pulled away. 'It's a weapon of man's destruction.'

She groaned. 'You can always kiss me to shut me up. I can't promise I won't blow you away, though.'

He mumbled something low and pithy under this breath. And then he kissed her.

A long while later, stretched out alongside Marco's warm length on the back seat of the car, she finally acknowledged her feelings.

She was happy. It was a happiness doomed to disaster and a short lifespan, but no matter how delusional she wanted it to last a little while longer.

Glancing down, she noticed Marco's wallet had dropped onto the floor of the car. Spying a picture peeking out, she picked up the wallet and peered closer.

The long, unruly hair was unfamiliar, as was the small go-kart in the background. But the determination and fierce pride in those hazel eyes looked familiar.

'This picture of you is adorable. Now I know what your children will look like.' She tried not to let the pain of that thought show on her face. 'I bet they'll be racers just like you and Rafael.'

Marco stiffened, his eyes growing cold and bleak. 'There won't be any children.'

The granite-like certainty in his voice chilled her soul. 'Why do you say that?'

For a long, endless moment he didn't answer. Then he took the wallet from her. Reaching for his trousers, he opened the car door, stepped out and pulled them on.

'Come with me.'

Despite already missing his arms around her, she sat up. 'Where are we going?'

The look in his eyes grew bleaker. 'Not far. Put your clothes on. I don't want to get distracted.'

She was all for distracting him if it meant he wouldn't look so cold and forbidding. But she did as he said.

Marco led her to the far side of the garage. Keying in a security code, he threw open the door and stepped inside, pulling her behind him.

With a flick of a switch, light bathed the room. Sasha looked around and gasped at the contents of many glass cabinets.

'These are all yours?' she whispered. Walking forward she opened the first cabinet and lifted the first trophy.

'Sí.' Marco's voice was husky with emotion. 'I started racing when I was five.'

There were more trophies than she could count, filling four huge cabinets. 'I know.'

He walked to the farthest cabinet and picked up the lone trophy standing in a case by itself. 'This was my last trophy.'

'You never told me why you gave up racing,' she murmured.

When he tensed even more, she went to him and grasped his balled fists.

'Tell me what happened.'

His eyes bored into hers, as if judging her to see if he could trust her with his pain. After an eternity his hand loosened enough to grasp hers.

'I got my first contract to race when I was eighteen. By twenty-one I'd won two championships and acquired a degree in engineering. I was on the list of every team, and I had the choice of picking which team to drive for. A week after I signed for my dream team I met Angelique Santoro. I was twenty-four, and foolishly believed in love at first sight. And even by then I'd had my fill of paddock bunnies. She was…different. Smart, sexy, exciting—far older than her twenty-five years. All I wanted to do was race and be with her. She convinced me to sack my manager and take her on instead. Six months later we were engaged and she was pregnant.'

A shiver of dread raced over Sasha. Deep inside her chest a ball of pain, buried but not forgotten, tightened.

There won't be any children.

'You didn't want the baby?' she whispered in horror.

He laughed. A harsh, tortured sound that twisted her heart. 'I wanted it more than I'd ever wanted anything in my life.'

Sasha frowned. 'But…what happened?'

'I rearranged my whole life around that promise of a family. I designed the *Casa de Leon* track so I could train there, instead of going away to train at other tracks. My parents moved here. My mother was ecstatic at becoming a grandparent.'

The note of pain through his voice rocked her.

'Angelique wasn't satisfied?'

'She wholeheartedly agreed with everything. Until I crashed.'

Her hand tightened around his. 'I don't understand. Your crash was serious, yes, but nothing you couldn't come back from.'

'I was in a coma for nine days. The team hired someone else to replace me when the doctors told my parents and Angelique it was unlikely I'd race again.'

'They must have been devastated for you.'

'My parents were.'

Sadness touched her soul. 'I'm sorry. I can't imagine what you must have gone through.'

He slid a finger under her chin and lifted her face to his, an echo of pain in his eyes. 'Nor would I want you to. But this…' he pulled her closer, his gaze softening a touch '…this helps.'

With a smile, she lifted her mouth to his. 'I'm glad.'

Their kiss was gentle, a soothing balm on his turbulent revelations.

When they parted, she glanced again at the trophies. 'Is that why you don't let anyone in here? Because it reminds you that your racing career is over?'

'When I accepted that part of my life was over I locked them away.' He pulled her away from the cabinet.

'Wait. You said your parents were devastated? What about Angelique?'

He stiffened again, his gaze turning hooded as he thrust his hands into his pockets. 'When it turned out I was destined for a job designing cars instead of racing them, she lost interest,' he said simply, but his oblique tone told a different story.

'That's not all, is it?'

Pain washed over his face before he could mask it. 'Before I crashed Angelique was almost three months pregnant. When I woke from my coma she was no longer pregnant.'

Sasha's horrified gasp echoed through the room. 'She had an abortion?'

His eyes turned almost black with pain. '*Sí.* Two months later she married my ex-team boss.'

A wave of horror washed over her. 'Are you even sure she was pregnant in the first place?' Considering how heartless the woman had been, Sasha wouldn't be surprised if she'd faked the pregnancy.

Marco's movements were uncharacteristically jerky as he

reached for his wallet. Beneath the photo, a small grey square slid out. In the light of the trophy room Sasha saw the outline of a tiny body in a pre-natal scan.

Tears gathered in her eyes and fell before she could stop them. With shaking hands she took the picture from him, the memory of her own loss striking into her heart so sharply she couldn't breathe.

'I was there the day this was taken. The thing was, all along I suspected Angelique was capable of that. She was extremely ruthless—driven to the point of obsession. But since she channelled all that into being my manager I chose to see it as something else.'

'Love?' she suggested huskily.

His jaw tightened. 'I blinded myself to her true colours. My mother tried to warn me, but I wouldn't listen to her. I almost cut her out of my life because of Angelique.' He sucked in a harsh breath. 'I lost my child…she lost her grandchild…because I chose to bury my head in the sand. She was devastated, and I don't think she really got over the damage I did to our family.'

Brushing a hand across her cheek, she asked, 'Why do you keep this?'

Marco took the scan and placed it back in his wallet. 'I failed to protect my daughter. This reminds me never to fail my family again.'

CHAPTER ELEVEN

MARCO left again the next day and didn't return for another two. When he returned Sasha met him in the hallway. His dragged her into his study and proceeded to kiss her with brutal need.

His confession in the garage had afforded her a glimpse into the man he was today. She now truly understood why he was so ferociously protective of Rafael. And why she couldn't afford for him to find out the true depth of her feelings.

Taking a deep breath, she forced herself to vocalise what she'd been too afraid to say over the phone the night before.

'Marco, I think I should leave. You can stay in Barcelona and not keep flying back here to see me. I can use the race track back home to train.'

His face clouded in a harsh frown. 'What the hell are you talking about?' Roughly he pulled her into his arms and kissed her again. 'You're not going anywhere.'

She tried to pull back but he held her easily. 'But—'

His smile was strained through tiredness. 'Rafael woke briefly last night. Only for a few minutes. But he appeared lucid, and he recognised me.' The relief in his voice was palpable.

Sasha smiled. 'I'm glad. But I think that's even more of a reason for you to stay in Barcelona. What if he wakes again when you're not there?'

Setting her free, he stabbed a hand through his hair. 'He's been moved to a private suite and I've set up video conferencing so I have a live feed into his room. Nothing will happen to him without my knowledge. I've also hired extra round-the-clock staff for when he comes home—including that nurse who was fired from the hospital in Budapest. So, you see, I'm not a total ass.'

'I know you're not. But you're splitting yourself in two when it's really Rafael who needs you most now.'

'Maybe I want to put my needs ahead of Rafael's for once in my life.' He threw his hands up in the air. 'What exactly do you want from me, Sasha?'

She was unprepared for the question. But she had one of her own burning at the back of her mind.

'What do *you* want from *me*? What is the real reason you want me to stay here? Am I here just so you can have sex on tap or is this something more…?' She faltered to a halt, too afraid to voice the words traipsing through her mind.

His eyes narrowed. 'I hardly think this is the time to be having a *where is this relationship going?* conversation.'

'Is there ever a right time? Besides, you don't *do* relationships, remember?'

He shrugged off his jacket and flung it onto a nearby chair. 'I want you here with me. Isn't that enough?' he rasped.

Another question she wasn't prepared for. Not because she didn't know the answer. It was because she knew the answer was *no*. Wanting was no longer enough. She was in love with Marco: with the boy whose heart had been shredded by a heartless woman and the formidable man who'd loved his unborn child so completely he'd closed his heart to any emotion.

She loved him. And it scared the hell out of her. The urge to retreat stabbed through her. Marco's obvious reluctance to discuss their relationship frightened her. But looking at him, his face haggard, his hands clenched on the desk in front of him, she knew she couldn't leave. Not just yet. Not when he was so worried about Rafael.

'I'll stay,' she said.

Naked relief reflected in his eyes. *'Gracias.'* He pulled her into his arms. 'Don't mention leaving again. Even the mere thought makes me want to hurl something.'

She hated herself for the thrill of pleasure that surged through her. 'It was for your own good—even if you don't want to see it.' And not just for Marco's sake. She had to find the strength to walk away. Because the longer she stayed, the more she risked losing everything.

'If you want suggestions on what's good for me, I have several ideas—' He stopped and cursed when his phone started ringing.

'Before you start hurling things, I'll remove myself to the garage. Your '65 Chevelle Impala's chrome finish needs polishing.'

'It also has extra wide front seats, if I recall.'

Desire weakened her. 'Marco…'

'Fine. But before you go—'

He plastered his lips against hers and proceeded to show her just how foolish her decision to leave had been.

By the time Sasha stumbled from the study she knew her heart was in serious trouble.

Marco threw himself into his seat two days later and barely stopped himself from punching a hole in the wall behind him.

Even though she'd changed her mind about leaving, Marco had sensed a withdrawal in Sasha he couldn't shake. It was almost as if Rafael's impending emergence from his coma had put a strain between them.

But why? If there was nothing between them Sasha should be happy that Rafael was recovering. Unless…? The thought that Sasha had feelings for Rafael after all sent a wave of anger and jealousy through him.

No. He dismissed the thought.

She'd listened to him bare his soul, held him in her arms as he'd relived Angelique's betrayal. Sasha had shed tears for him; he refused to believe the raw pain he'd seen in her eyes wasn't real.

But he couldn't deny something was wrong.

Only when they made love, when he held her afterwards, did he feel he had the real Sasha back. Even now, mere hours before she was due to leave for London, she'd locked herself away in his garage, hell-bent on restoring his vintage cars to even more pristine condition than they'd originally been in. While he sat here, grappling with confusion and a hunger so relentless he was surprised he didn't spontaneously combust from want.

No. It was more than want. This craving for Sasha, whether she was within arm's reach or he was in Barcelona, went beyond anything he'd ever known. The few times he'd contemplated whether it would be better if she wasn't at the villa at all he'd felt a wrench so deep it had shaken him.

Angelique had never made him feel like this, even though at the time he'd thought he would never yearn for another woman the way he'd yearned for her.

What he felt for Sasha was different...deeper...purer...

Marco stiffened, the breath trapped in his chest as he tried to get to grips with his feelings. But the more he tried to unravel the unfamiliar feeling, the more chaotic and frantic it grew.

He glanced out of his study window towards his garage. The feeling that she was slipping through his fingers wouldn't fade. But he couldn't deal with it now. There were too many loose ends left to tie up.

As if on cue, his phone rang. With a muttered curse, he picked it up.

All the way to his suite Sasha forced herself to breathe. Despite the cold lump of stone in her stomach, she needed to do this. She couldn't continue to string things along any longer.

She entered the suite and heard the shower running. Without pausing, she crossed the room and slid open the door.

Water streamed off Marco's naked, powerful body. The need that slammed through her threatened to weaken her resolve. It took several seconds before she could speak.

'Marco, I...I've decided...I'm not coming back here after the next race.'

He whirled about, looked stricken for a moment, then his jaw clenched. 'I thought we had this conversation already.'

Even now, with the wrenching pain of losing him coursing through her, she couldn't resist the intense pull of desire that watching the water cascade over his body brought.

She steeled herself against it. 'I tried to talk. You laid down the law.'

He snapped a towel off the heated rack and stepped from the shower. 'You timed it perfectly, didn't you?'

'Excuse me?'

'Your exit strategy. At first I didn't want to believe it, but now it makes perfect sense.'

She frowned. 'Perfect sense… What are you talking about?'

'You can drop the pretence. I had a call twenty minutes ago. From Raven Blass.'

Her eyes widened in surprise. 'Raven? Why—?'

'She's in Barcelona. She wants to see Rafael. I gave the hospital permission to let her see him, but funnily enough she was more worried about how *you* would feel about her visit.'

'Marco—'

'Apparently you're very *territorial* about Rafael. She said something about warning Rafael to stay away from her the day he crashed?'

'That wasn't how it was—'

He tied the towel around his trim waist. 'What was the plan? Use me as a stopgap until Rafael was on his feet, then go back to him?'

'Of course not!'

'You started withdrawing from me the moment I told you Rafael was about to wake up. Well, I'm glad to have been of service. But if you have any designs on my brother, kill them now. He won't like soiled goods.'

She flinched and bit back her gasp. For a moment he appeared to regret his words, then his expression hardened again.

'Wow. Okay, I guess your mind's made up.'

'I mean it, Sasha. Come anywhere near Rafael and I'll crush you like a bug.'

Pain congealed into a crushing weight in her chest. 'I suspected this, and I see I was right. Rafael will always come first with you—no matter how much you protest about putting yourself first. I just hope you don't have to give up something you really want one day.'

He frowned. 'There's nothing I want more than my family safe.'

'Well, that says it all, doesn't it?'

Whirling, she hurried from the room, cursing the stupid tears that welled up in her eyes.

In her room, she grabbed her suitcase and stuffed her belongings into it. She was snapping it shut when her door flew open.

'What are you doing?'

'Leaving. *Obviously.*'

'Your flight is not for another four hours.'

She picked her case off the bed. 'Oh? And what? You want one last shag for old times' sake?'

His eyes darkened in a familiar way even as his jaw clenched.

A stunned laugh escaped her. 'Let me get this straight. You want more sex with me even though I'm "soiled goods" you wouldn't let your own brother touch?'

Dull colour swam into his cheeks. 'Don't put it like that.'

'You know when I said you weren't an ass? I was stupendously wrong! You're the biggest ass in the universe.' She stalked towards the door.

'Sasha—'

'And to think I fooled myself into thinking I was in love with you. You don't deserve love. And you certainly don't deserve mine!'

Had she looked back as she sped through the door, pleased with herself for not breaking down in front of him, she would have seen his stunned face, his ashen pallor.

Sasha flew home to Kent after the Indian Grand Prix, one step closer to cementing the Constructors' Championship.

Returning home for the first time in months felt bittersweet. Glancing round the familiar surroundings of the home she'd grown up in, she wanted to burst into tears. Pictures of her father graced the mantel. A wooden cabinet in the dining room held their trophies. They weren't as numerous as Marco's, but she was proud of every single one of them. Unlike Marco, who'd chosen to hide his away the way he'd chosen to close off his heart…

But had he? He'd shown her that he would fight to the death to protect his family. Didn't that prove it was *her* who wasn't worth fighting for? The thought hurt more than she could bear.

With an angry hand she dashed away the tears. She refused to dwell on him. Her only goal now was finishing the season. She couldn't summon the appropriate enthusiasm for next year.

Wearily, she trudged to the kitchen and put on the kettle. Mrs Miller, her next door neighbour, had texted to let her know the fridge was fully stocked.

Sasha opened the fridge, caught a whiff of cheese and felt her stomach lurch violently. She barely made it to the bathroom seconds before emptying the contents of her stomach. Rinsing her mouth, she decided to forgo the tea in favour of sleep. Dragging herself to the shower, she washed off the grime of her transatlantic flight and fell into bed.

The stomach bug she suspected she'd caught in India, along with half of the team, didn't go away immediately, but by the time she arrived in Brazil three and a half weeks later she was in full health.

And three points away from securing the championship.

São Paolo was vibrant and exhilarating. The pit was abuzz with the excitement of the season's final race, and Team Espiritu even more so with a potential championship win only a few short hours away.

Sasha had taken the coward's way and hidden in her hotel room until the last minute, in case she bumped into Marco. In Abu Dhabi she'd declined his invitation to an after-race party on his sprawling yacht. It seemed he was back to entertaining dignitaries and A-list celebrities with barely a blink in her direction.

Whereas she…she just wanted the season to be over.

The joy had gone out of racing.

With a sharp pang she realised Marco had been right—her guilt about her father had blinded her to the fact that she didn't need to prove to anyone that she was good enough. Nor did she need to defend Jack Fleming's integrity. With her deeper integration and final acceptance into the team she'd discovered that most people remembered Jack Fleming as the great driver he'd been. Her guilt lingered, but she would deal with that later.

First she had to get through the press interviews before and after the race.

She spotted Tom heading her way as she was pulling on her jumpsuit. She winced at the sensitivity of her breasts as the Velcro tightened over them.

She paused, then suddenly was scrambling madly for dates, calculating frantically and coming up short every time. Panic seized her.

'Are you all right? You've gone pale. Here—have some water.'

Tom poured water into a plastic cup and handed it to her. His attitude had undergone a drastic change since she'd become involved with Marco. Snarkily, Sasha wondered whether he'd go back to being insufferable once he found out she and Marco were no longer together.

'It's the heat,' she replied, setting the cup aside. 'I'm fine,' she stressed when he continued to peer at her in concern.

'Okay. Your last interview is with local TV.' He rolled his eyes. 'It's that smarmy one who interviewed you in Singapore. I'd cut him out of the schedule, but since we're on his home turf we don't have any choice. Don't worry. If he looks as if he's straying into forbidden territory I'll stop him.'

He went on to list the other interviewers, but Sasha was only half listening. She'd finally worked out her period dates and breathed a sigh of relief. She'd had her last albeit brief period just before she'd left Leon. And her cycle was erratic at the best of times.

Reassured, she followed Tom around to the paddock and spoke to the journalists.

The race itself was uneventful. With her eight-second lead unchallenged after the first six laps she cruised to victory, securing the fastest lap ever set on the Interlagos circuit. She managed to keep a smile plastered on her face all through the celebrations and the myriad interviews that followed, sighing with relief as she entered the team's hospitality suite for her last interview.

Despite having done dozens of interviews, she still suffered an attack of nerves whenever a camera was trained on her. And, unlike nerves during a race, interview nerves never worked to her advantage.

'Don't worry, Miss Fleming. It will be all right.'

The note of insincerity in the interviewer's thick accent should have been her first warning.

The first few questions were okay. Then, 'How does it feel to be dating the team boss? Has it earned you any advantages?'

From the corner of her eye she saw Tom surge from his seat. Her 'no comment' made him relax a little.

'After winning the Constructors' Championship, surely your seat for next year is secured?'

'No comment.'

He shrugged. 'How about your ex, Derek Mahoney? Have you heard he's making a comeback to racing?'

Sasha tensed. 'No, I haven't heard.'

'He gave us an interview this morning. And he mentioned something quite interesting.'

Icy dread crept up her spine. 'Whatever it is, I'm sure it has nothing to do with me.'

'On the contrary, it has everything to do with you.'

Her interviewer rubbed his chin in a way that was probably supposed to make him appear smart. It only confirmed the slimeball he really was.

'You see, Mr Mahoney claims you were pregnant with his child when you broke up, and that you deliberately crashed to lose the baby because you didn't want a child to hamper your career. What's your response to that?'

The room swayed around her. Vaguely she heard Tom shouting at the cameraman to stop filming. Inside she was frozen solid, too afraid to move. The buzz in the room grew louder. Someone grasped her arm and frogmarched her into another room. The sole occupant, a waitress cleaning a table, looked from her to the TV and quickly made herself scarce.

'Sasha... I... God, this is a mess,' Tom stuttered. 'Will you be all right? I need to secure that footage...'

'Please, go. I...I'll be fine,' she managed through frozen lips.

He hurriedly retreated and she was alone.

Dropping her head between her thighs, she tried to breathe evenly, desperately willing herself not to pass out. The TV hummed in the background but she didn't have the strength to walk over to turn it off.

Oh, God, how had Derek found out? Not that it mattered now. Her secret was out. Out there for the whole world to pore over...

Tears welled in her eyes. Derek was all about causing maximum damage. But she'd never dreamed he'd sink this low.

The door flew open and Marco walked in.

Her gaze collided with his, and every single thing she'd told herself over the last three weeks flew out of the door.

He'd lost weight. The gap at the collar of his light blue shirt showed more of his collarbones and his jacket hung looser. But he was just as arresting, just as breathlessly beautiful, and her heart leapt with shameless joy at the sight of him.

'I need to talk to you,' he said tautly, his gaze roving intensely over her before capturing hers again.

She licked her dry lips. 'I...I need to tell you...' How could she tell him? She'd never vocalised her pain, never told another human being.

'What is it?' He came over and took her hands. 'Whatever it is, tell me. I can handle it.'

That gave her a modicum of strength. 'You promise?'

'*Sí.* I have a few things I need to tell you too, *mi corazón*. The things I said in Leon...' He paused and shook his head, a look of regret in his eyes. 'You were right. I'm an ass.'

'I didn't...' *I didn't mean it*, she started to confess, but her eyes had strayed to the TV. There, like a vivid recurring nightmare, her interview was being replayed.

Seeing her distraction, Marco followed her gaze.

Just in time to hear the interviewer's damning question.

Marco dropped her hands faster than hot coals and surged to his feet. '*No!* It's a lie. Isn't it, Sasha? *Isn't it?*' he shouted when she couldn't speak.

'I...'

He paled, his cheekbones standing out against his stark face as he stepped back from her.

'Marco, please—it wasn't like that.' She finally found her voice. But it was too late.

He'd taken several more steps backwards, as if he couldn't stand to breathe the same air as her.

'Did you race knowing you were pregnant?' he insisted, his voice harsh.

'Not the day Derek's talking about—'

'But you *did* race knowing you were pregnant?'

'I suspected I was—'

'Dios mío!'

'I'd already lost the baby when I crashed. That was *why* I crashed! Racing was all I knew. After the doctor told me I'd lost the baby I didn't know what else to do.'

'So you got straight back in your car? You didn't even take time to mourn the loss of your child?' he condemned in chilling tones.

Somehow she found the strength to stand and face him. 'The doctor said it wasn't my fault. The pregnancy wasn't viable to begin with. But I still cried myself to sleep every night for years afterwards. If you're asking if I carry a picture of a scan to punish myself with, or as an excuse to push people away, then no, I don't. She lives in my heart—'

"She?" His voice was a tortured rasp, his fists clenching and unclenching and his throat working as he paled even more.

Tears spilled from her eyes and she nodded. 'Mine was a girl too. She lives in my heart and that's where I choose to remember her. You say you don't live in the past, but that's exactly what you're doing. You're judging *me* by what happened to you ten years ago.'

He inhaled sharply. 'And you've proved to me just how far you'll go. I told you about Angelique, about my child, and you said nothing. Because a small thing like a lost pregnancy is less important to you than your next race, isn't it?'

She swayed as pain clamped her chest in a crushing vice. 'You know why I wanted to race!'

'I was a fool to believe you were trying to preserve the memory of your father. You were really just seeking to further your own agenda.'

Pain arrowed through her. 'Don't pretend you don't think he was guilty.'

'I said he was *found* guilty. I didn't say I agreed with the verdict.'

'But—'

He slashed a hand through her words. 'I had my lawyers investigate the case. Some of the testimony didn't add up. If your father had spent less time feeling sorry for himself and more time getting his lawyers to concentrate on his case he'd have realised that. That's one of the things I came here to tell you.'

Tears stung the backs of her eyes, her throat clogging with unspoken words. 'Marco, please—can't we talk about this?'

He gave a single, finite shake of his head. 'I'm not interested in anything you have to say. I'm only grateful I never made you pregnant. I don't think I could survive another child of mine being so viciously denied life for the sake of ruthless ambition.'

Her insides froze as his words cut across her skin.

With one last condemning look he headed towards the door. Panic seized her. 'Marco!'

He stilled but didn't turn around, one hand on the doorknob. 'What else did you come to say to me?'

The cold malice in his eyes when he turned around made her heart clench.

'I sold the team six weeks ago. In Korea. The paperwork was finalised today. As of one hour ago your contract is null and void.'

CHAPTER TWELVE

SHE was pregnant with Marco's child. Sasha had been certain of it almost as soon as Marco had walked out on her in São Paolo. Taking the pregnancy test once she'd returned home had only established what she'd known in her heart.

There was no doubt in her mind that she would tell him he was about to become a father. The only problem was when.

He'd made his feelings clear. Her own emotions were too raw for her to face another showdown with Marco. She doubted he would believe whatever she had to tell him anyway.

Gentle fingers stroked over her belly. The doctor had confirmed today that she was almost three months pregnant. Her fingers stilled. Angelique had terminated Marco's child at three months. Sadness welled inside her as she recalled Marco's face when he'd shown her his scan.

Making up her mind before she lost the courage, she dug out her phone. Her fingers shook as she pressed the numbers.

'*Si?*' came the deep voice.

'Marco, it's me.'

Taut silence.

'I know you don't want to speak to me…but there's something I need to tell you.'

'I'm no longer in the motor racing business, so you're wasting your time.' The line went dead.

Sasha stared at the phone, anger and pain churning through her. *'Ass.'*

She threw the phone down, vowing to make Marco beg before she let him anywhere near his child.

Two days later Sasha was standing at her fridge stacking groceries when she heard the agonisingly familiar sound of helicopter rotorblades. The aircraft flew directly over her small cottage before landing in a field half a mile away.

Even though she forced herself to finish her task, every sense was attuned to the knock that came less than five minutes later.

Heart hammering, she opened her door to find Marco standing there, tall, dark and windswept.

'You know you'll have my neighbours dining out on your spectacular entrance for years, don't you? What the hell are you doing here anyway? I recall you wanting nothing to do with me.'

Hazel eyes locked on hers, the look in them almost imploring. 'Invite me in, Sasha.'

'I don't invite heartless bloodsuckers into my home. You can stay right where you are. Better yet, jump back into your vampire-mobile and leave.'

'I'm not leaving until you hear what I have to say. I don't care what your neighbours think, but I get the feeling *you* do. There's a blue-haired one staring at us right now.' Brazen, he waved at Mrs Miller, who shamelessly waved back and kept right on staring at them.

Firming her lips, Sasha stepped back and waved him in. 'You think you're very clever, don't you?'

Expecting a quick comeback, she turned from shutting the door to find him staring at her, a tormented grimace on his face.

'No, I don't think I'm clever at all. In fact, right now, I'm the stupidest person I know.'

Her mouth dropped open.

His grimace deepened. 'Yes, I know. Shocker.'

'Marco…' She stopped and finally did what she'd been dying to do since he knocked on her door. She let her eyes devour him. Let her heart delight in the sheer magnificent sight of him. He went straight to her head. Made her sway where she stood.

He stared right back at her, a plethora of emotions she was

too afraid to name passing over his face. He opened his mouth a couple of times but, seemingly losing his nerve to speak, cast his gaze around her small living room, over the pictures and racing knick-knacks she and her father had accumulated over the years.

Finally he dug into his jacket pocket. 'This is for you.'

Sasha took the papers. 'What are these?'

'Signed affidavits from two former drivers who swear your father wasn't involved in the fraud. He was the fall guy.'

Hands shaking, she read through the documents. 'How...? Why...?' Tears clogged her throat, making the words difficult to utter. Finally she could clear her father's name.

'The how doesn't matter. The why is because you deserve to know.'

She didn't realise she was crying until the first teardrop landed on her hand. Sucking in a sustaining breath, she swiped at her cheeks. 'I...I really don't know what to say. After what happened...' She glanced down at the papers again and swallowed. 'Thank you, Marco,' she said huskily.

'De nada,' he replied hoarsely.

'You didn't have to deliver it in person, though.'

His watchful look intensified. 'I didn't. But I needed the excuse to see you.'

'Why?' she whispered, too afraid to hope.

He swallowed. 'Rafael woke up—really woke up yesterday.'

Her heart lurched. 'Is he okay?'

Marco nodded. 'I went to see him this morning. He told me what happened in Budapest.'

Sasha sighed. 'I know it was stupid, but I lost it when I found out what Rafael was doing.'

'You mean deliberately using your friendship to make Raven jealous?'

She nodded. 'I think she was smitten with Rafael when she first joined the team. That changed when she found out he'd dated most of the women in the paddock. She refused to have anything to do with him after that.'

Marco pursed his lips. 'And he, of course, found it a challenge when she kept refusing him. Why didn't you tell me?' he demanded.

'You told me the significance of your mother's ring. I didn't think you needed to know Rafael was intending to use it to...'

'Get lucky?' He grimaced, then sobered. 'He's over that now, I think. He's seems different—more...mature. I think the accident was a wake-up call for him.'

His eyes locked on her, their expression so bleak it broke her heart.

'For me too. You were right.'

'I was?'

He moved towards her suddenly. '*Sí*. I was living in the past. I knew it even before you left Leon. I knew it when I came to see you in São Paolo. Hearing Rafael tell me what I already knew—how great you are, how much of a friend you'd been to him...' He stopped and swallowed. 'Did I mention I'm the stupidest person I know right now?'

'Um, you may have.'

'What I said in São Paolo was unforgivable...' His anxious gaze snared hers. 'I was in shock, but I never should've said what I did. I'm sorry you lost your baby. I think you would've made a brilliant mother.'

'You do?'

'*Sí*. I saw how the Children of Bravery Awards affected you. You held it together despite your pain. Watching you on stage with the kids made me wish my child had had a mother like you. At least then she would've had a chance.'

Tears filled her eyes. 'Oh, Marco...' She could barely speak past the lump in her throat.

Another grimace slashed his face. 'I've made you cry again.' He sat next to her and gently brushed away her tears. 'This wasn't what I intended by coming here.'

'Why did you come here, Marco?'

He sucked in a huge breath. 'To tell you I love you. And to beg your forgiveness.'

'You love me?'

He gave a jerky nod. 'It ripped me apart to learn I'd had your love and lost it because I'd been so stupid. When you called two days ago—'

'When you hung up on me?'

'I panicked. The hospital had just called about Rafael. I thought you knew and were calling to ask to see him.' He frowned. 'Why *did* you call?'

'I had something to tell you. When you hung up on me I wrote a letter instead.'

'A letter?'

'Well, it was more like a list.'

She'd done it to stop herself from crying—something she couldn't seem to stop doing lately.

Reaching into her pocket, she pulled it out and held it towards him. 'Here.'

He stared at the paper but didn't take it, his face ashen. 'Is forgiveness anywhere on that list, by any chance?'

Her gaze sharpened on him. 'Forgiveness?'

'Yes. Forgiveness of judgemental bastards who don't know the special gift of love and beauty and goodness when it's handed to them.'

'Er...' She glanced down at the list, her thundering heartbeat echoing loudly in her ears. 'No. But then I've only had two days to work on it.'

Dropping down on his haunches, he cupped her face in his hands. 'Then consider this a special request, *por favor*. I know I have a lot of grovelling to do for judging you harshly from the beginning.'

'You were hurting. And you were right. I *was* acting out of guilt.'

'No. You were doing whatever it took for you to move on— whereas I let one stumbling block shatter me. I resented you for that.'

'The blows you were dealt were enough to knock anyone sideways.'

'But I let it colour my judgement. I told myself I had recovered, that I didn't care, but I did. Do you know that until you came to Leon I hadn't entered that garage in over ten years? You opened my eyes to what a barren life I'd led until then.'

'Look at the letter, Marco.'

He inhaled sharply and stood. 'No. If you're going to condemn me I'd rather hear it from you.'

'You might want to sit down.'

He stuffed his fingers into his coat pockets, but not before she caught the trembling of his hands.

'Just tell me.'

'Fine. But if you faint from shock don't expect me to help you. You're too big—'

When he made an incoherent sound racked with pain, she unfolded the paper.

Anxiety coursed through her. He'd said he loved her, but what if Marco truly didn't want another child? What if the loss of his unborn child had been too great a pain for him ever to move on from?

'Sasha, *por favor.*'

'That's the second time you've said please in the last five minutes,' she whispered.

When his eyes grew dark, she read aloud. *'"Marco, you were an ass for hanging up on me but I think you should know—"'* She looked up from the sheet. *'"You're going to become a father."'*

For a full minute he didn't move. Didn't breathe, didn't blink. Then he stumbled into the chair. His hands visibly shook when he reached out and cupped her cheek. 'Sasha. Please tell me this isn't a dream,' he rasped.

'This isn't a dream. I'm pregnant with your child.'

A look of complete reverence settled over his face before his eyes dropped to her still-flat stomach.

'Are you okay? Is everything all right?' he demanded.

'You mean with the baby?'

'With both of you.'

'Yes. I saw the doctor. Everything is fine. Does that mean you want the baby?'

'*Mi corazón*, you've given me a second chance I never would've been brave enough to take on my own. I may have burned my bridges with you, but, yes, I want this baby.' His eyes dropped to her stomach, and lingered. '*Por favor*, can I touch?'

Sweet surprise rocked through her. 'You want to touch my belly?'

'If you'll allow me?'

'You know the baby isn't any larger than your thumb right now, don't you?'

'*Sí*, but my heart wants what it wants. Please?'

Renewed tears clogged her throat as she nodded and unbuttoned her jeans.

Warm fingers caressed her belly. Watching his face, she felt the breath snag in her chest at the sheer joy exhibited there. Then his eyes locked on hers and his fingers slid under her sweater, heating her bare flesh.

Her heart kicked, the fierce love she felt for this man and for her baby making her throat clog with tears. Reluctantly she withdrew from his seductive warmth. 'Marco, I haven't finished reading the letter.'

A look of uncertainty entered his eyes. 'I know what a hard bargain you can drive. Is there any room for negotiation?'

'You need to hear what's in it first.'

He gave a reluctant nod, his joy fading a little.

'"*If it's a boy I would like to name him after my father. One of his names, at least.*"'

A quick nod met her request. 'It will be so.'

'"*I want our child to be born in Spain. Preferably in Leon.*"'

He swallowed hard. 'Agreed.'

She looked up from the paper. '"*I'd like to stay there after the baby's born. With you.*"'

His eyes widened and he stopped breathing. 'You want to stay in Leon? With me?'

Her heart in her throat, she nodded. 'Our child deserves two parents who don't live in separate countries.'

Disappointment fleeted over his face. 'You're right.'

'Our child also deserves parents who love each other.'

Pain darkened his eyes. 'I intend to do everything in my power to earn your love again, Sasha.'

She shrugged, her heart in her throat. 'You'll need to focus your energies on other things, Marco. Because I love you.'

He sucked in a breath. 'You...love me...?'

'Yes,' she reiterated simply. 'I knew in Leon, even though I'd convinced myself it wouldn't work.'

'I didn't exactly make it easy. I felt my life unravelling and I got desperate.'

Shock rocked through her. 'Was that why you sold the team?'

He grimaced. 'Rafael's accident and your near-collision in Korea convinced me it was time to get out of racing. But I managed to bulldoze my way through that too. I also may have left a tiny detail out regarding your firing.'

'Oh?'

'The sale contract included a stipulation that you were to have first refusal of the lead driver's seat. If you wanted it.'

Lifting loving hands, she cradled his face. 'Didn't you read Tom's press release last week?'

'What press release?'

'I've retired from motor racing.'

He frowned. 'What about your promise to your father?'

'He would've been proud that I helped you win the Constructors' Championship. But what he really wanted was for me to be happy.'

'And are you?'

'Tell me you love me again and I'll let you know.'

'I am deeply, insanely in love with you, Sasha Fleming, and I can't wait to make you mine.'

She flung the letter away and slid her arms around his neck. 'Then, yes, I'm ecstatically happy.'

EPILOGUE

'HAPPY birthday, *mi preciosa*.'

Sasha turned from where she'd been watching another stunning Leon sunset and tucked the blanket around their two-month-old baby.

'*Shh.* You'll wake him.'

Marco joined her at the crib. With a look of complete adoration on his face, he brushed a finger down his son's soft cheek. 'Jack Alessandro de Cervantes can sleep through a hurricane—just like his mother.' He pressed a kiss on his son's forehead, then held out his hand to her. 'Come with me.'

'Marco, you're not giving me another present? You've already given me six—oh, never mind.' By now she knew better than to dissuade her husband when he was on a mission. Today his mission was to shower her with endless gifts.

'*Sí*, now you're learning.'

As Marco led her to their bedroom she glanced down at the large square diamond ring he'd slid next to her seven-month-old wedding ring this morning. Not a week went by without Marco giving her a gift of some sort. Last week he'd presented her with the most darling chocolate Labradoodle puppy, and then grumbled when she'd immediately fallen in love with the dog.

'I hope it's not another diamond. There's only so much bling a girl can wear before she's asking for a mugging.'

'It's not a diamond. This present is much more...personal.'

He shut the door behind them, settled his hands on her hips and pulled her closer, his hazel eyes growing dramatically darker. 'The kind of *personal* that happens when you wear this T-shirt.'

'Why do you think I'm wearing it?'

He gave a low, sexy laugh. '*Dios*, you're merciless.'

'Only when it comes to you. Turning you on gives me a huge buzz.'

Stretching up, she wrapped her arms around his neck, luxuriating in their long kiss until she reluctantly pulled away.

At his protest, she shook her head. 'I have something to show you before we get too carried away.'

Reaching towards her bedside table, she handed him a single piece of heavily embossed paper.

He read through the document before glancing up at her. 'It's finalised?'

Happiness burst through her chest. 'Yes. The mayor's office sent over confirmation this afternoon. I'm officially patron of the De Cervantes Children's Charity. My programme to help disadvantaged kids who're interested in racing is a go!'

His devastating smile held pride even as he sighed. 'Between that and you being spokeswoman for women motor racers, I see my cunning plan to keep you busy in my bed having babies fast disappearing.'

Her smack on his arm was rewarded with a kiss on her willing mouth.

He sobered. 'Are you sure you don't want to go back to racing? You know you'd have my support in that too.'

Sasha blinked eyes prickling with tears and pressed her mouth against his. 'Thank you, but that part of my life is over. The chance to work with children is another dream come true. As for making more babies with you—it's my number one priority. Right up there with loving you for ever.'

His eyes darkened. 'I love you too, *mi corazón*.'

'Enough to take advantage of the instruction on my T-shirt?' she asked saucily.

With a growl, he tumbled her back onto the bed and proceeded to demonstrate just how good he was at taking instruction.

* * * * *

Mills & Boon® Hardback

December 2012

ROMANCE

A Ring to Secure His Heir	Lynne Graham
What His Money Can't Hide	Maggie Cox
Woman in a Sheikh's World	Sarah Morgan
At Dante's Service	Chantelle Shaw
At His Majesty's Request	Maisey Yates
Breaking the Greek's Rules	Anne McAllister
The Ruthless Caleb Wilde	Sandra Marton
The Price of Success	Maya Blake
The Man From her Wayward Past	Susan Stephens
Blame it on the Bikini	Natalie Anderson
The English Lord's Secret Son	Margaret Way
The Secret That Changed Everything	Lucy Gordon
Baby Under the Christmas Tree	Teresa Carpenter
The Cattleman's Special Delivery	Barbara Hannay
Secrets of the Rich & Famous	Charlotte Phillips
Her Man In Manhattan	Trish Wylie
His Bride in Paradise	Joanna Neil
Christmas Where She Belongs	Meredith Webber

MEDICAL

From Christmas to Eternity	Caroline Anderson
Her Little Spanish Secret	Laura Iding
Christmas with Dr Delicious	Sue MacKay
One Night That Changed Everything	Tina Beckett